THE

MIDDLE

GROUND

THE MIDDLE GROUND

STORIES

JEFF EWING

Library and Archives Canada Cataloguing in Publication

Ewing, Jeff, 1956-, author
     The middle ground : stories / Jeff Ewing.

Issued in print and electronic formats.
ISBN 978-1-77538-130-3 (softcover).--ISBN 978-1-77538-131-0 (MOBI).--
ISBN 978-1-77538-132-7 (EPUB).--ISBN 978-1-77538-133-4 (AZW)

     I. Title.

PS3605.W56M53 2019   813'.6   C2018-903325-8
                                            C2018-903326-6

Printed in the United States of America

Designed by Into the Void

www.intothevoidmagazine.com

For Diane and Romy

CONTENTS

—Will you always remember me?

—Always.

—Will you remember me a year from now?

—Yes, I will.

—Will you remember me two years from now?

—Yes, I will.

—Will you remember me five years from now?

—Yes, I will.

—Knock knock.

—Who's there?

—You see?

—DONALD BARTHELME, "Great Days"

Everything exists, everything is true, and the earth is only a little dust under our feet.

—W.B. YEATS, *The Celtic Twilight*

THE
MIDDLE
GROUND

TULE FOG

WHEN PEOPLE TALK ABOUT CALIFORNIA, they don't mean here. They're talking about somewhere else—Palm Springs, Yosemite, Venice Beach, the redwoods—places that make for a good postcard, places where it wouldn't be an insult to tell someone you wish they were there. The valley doesn't fit on the same map. It's flat and it's hot, and the ground under you feels like something dead you're walking on. In summer the news stations show people cooking eggs on the sidewalk, and the anchors laugh their asses off and shake their heads. In the winter it rains for a while, then the tule fog moves up from the river basins into town.

It starts slowly, the air thickening, visibility dropping, then it's just there, so thick you have to walk with your hands out in front of you, fingers waggling like tentacles. It brushes up against you, coming on to you. But here's the thing—and most people don't know this—the fog has a false bottom. It hangs just above the ground, leaving a foot-high gap between its ragged hem and the skin of the valley floor. And in that gap, quietly and nearly bloodlessly, worlds are born and lost.

I watch it come in, then make my way across town to the neighborhood where I grew up, a once-desirable part of town that's gotten long in the tooth. The roofs of the ranch houses sag on their rafters now that the kids are all gone and the heat and pressure they generated has been sapped out. I walk down too-familiar streets, the fog soaking my jeans, until I come to a weedy lot across from a tidy house with brown siding. Like a child with defective blocks, I start to rebuild.

I take the small slice of visible world and construct a plausible alternative. Cars roll by, legs scissor past, all of it moving slowly and tentatively in anticipation of my guiding hand. Voices and the sound of dishes being stacked filter in from a couple of streets over. Tonight, I think. This will be it.

There are six beers strapped across my chest in a bandolier. Once I settle in—my jacket rolled into a pillow, a silver space blanket spread out under me—I slide one out and pop the top. I listen to the report echo and note the sudden suspension of the small sounds you don't notice until they stop. After a minute they come back, and I register their return one by one—the crickets ticking off the temperature, a mouse or a lizard tunneling through the grass, a rattlesnake curling and uncurling, its blood thick and sluggish. The fog amplifies it all, gathers it in lovingly.

"I haven't slept in I don't know how long." A girl's voice, as tired sounding as she claims. "Right. You'll sleep . . . Come on. No. Come on . . . Why do I have to say it?"

I can see the tires of her car, the left front a little low, settled more than the others on the angled drive. Her feet emerge together, fall in unison onto the concrete and click off toward the house in impatience or anticipation. The door closes behind her with the same hollowness that her voice carries, compressed and EQed by the fog.

~

My high school girlfriend's room was just off the garage there, the same room whose window lights up now with the half-assed glow of a compact fluorescent bulb. Some nights I'd coast my car to the curb and knock on the window, and Lisa would let me in through the garage. We'd sit on her bed and make out or listen to music. That was more than enough at the time—just imagine. She'd put on something slow and trickly and we'd listen until the sky started to lighten, the horizon pulsing beyond her back fence. Then I'd get back in my car and drive home. The air was like something sweet melting as I breathed it in through the window, my body tired and still vibrating faintly.

~

It took some practice to learn to drink lying on my back. It's a talent, of sorts. Nothing I could get into college or a circus with, but useful all the same. Because it leads to this sense of the world above and the world below coming closer, hints of reconciliation. But there is also a pale overlay—like vellum on vellum—of something else, an uneasiness not far from fear. You can hear it in the click of shoes, the slow rhythmic tapping that gradually speeds up as it digs in.

Kids avoid my field; they think it's haunted. They see lights moving through the fog, growing brighter, dimming. It's just a joint or a cigarette, but they don't know that. They're kids. Unexplainable events are their gold standard. It's only later that mysteries stop being prizes, that we fight against them with everything we have.

⌒

When I'm making my way over here from the light rail station, I take a route planned carefully to avoid the house I grew up in. Partly because it's so run down now that I'm tempted to set fire to it, but mainly because it's impossible not to look out from the yard and see what I saw when I was a kid, when there was nothing but new roofs and promise all the way out as far as you could see, all the way to the crest of the mountains. The trees were all small, our size, and the breeze passing between the houses was soft and clean as the air from a dryer vent. Now it's sharp with dry rot and rank vegetation, and the mountains curl above the houses like an animal in mid-pounce.

I can't see the mountains at the moment. Sometimes you can't even see them in the daylight, but they're there, jagged pieces of the earth pushed up at the edge of the valley like teeth breaking through gums. They define us by contrast, and we exaggerate their majesty to temper our poor reflections. Every day people go up there from the valley, and they come back changed—they claim to take something away that they didn't go up with, even though it's just an hour's drive with no hardship to it. They're better people for the trip, with a clearer appreciation of their place in the world. I don't believe them, but I understand them. You couldn't live here long without telling yourself that kind of thing.

~

The radio coming from Lisa's former room sounds cheap and tinny, Ray Davies' voice brittle as an old polaroid. I hadn't pegged the girl for the classic rock type. Maybe it's the only station she gets.

Lisa had a small sub-collection of albums, stacked off to the side of her bed in their own little library, whose binding theme was the moon. You don't realize how many moon songs there are until you start grouping them like that. There are far more than necessary, probably because they don't take much work. You look up and there it is, that blue shining harvest honey moon. You scribble a couple of verses about how waxen and dermal the light is, hash out a chorus expressing your awe at the magnificence and complexity of the world, then you sit back and wait for the royalties to roll in.

The kids eat it up, they think that's romance. Which it is—for a time—and far be it from me to take that from them. But the moon's been in reach for a long time now, and it's tough to look up at it without thinking how we screwed ourselves when we stepped out onto it. How we went up there arrogant giants and came back petulant little shits.

~

A pickup slows and pulls to the curb. The door opens,

feet exit. I see cowboy boots. Not working boots, ma-
nure-splattered and wrinkled like pork rinds, but soft,
shiny boots. Street boots. The toes point in a little toward each other as though they're about to start arguing,
then they move off onto the curb and up the front steps
of the house. Toward the slash of yellow light slipping
out under the door, widening and spilling onto the stoop
as the door opens without the boots even having had to
knock. They've been expected.

A pair of bare feet slip over the threshold; the left
foot rubs against the swell of the opposite calf.

"I'm sorry."

"For what?"

"Whatever."

"You don't even know."

"No. But I'm sorry anyway."

I arc my empty beer can toward the house in a long,
looping shot. It bounces once and rattles into the gut-
ter. The four feet turn. The cowboy and the girl look out
across a billowing plateau so insubstantial it can't even
support second thoughts.

～

Three doors down to the right is the house where my
friend Tim used to live. We were in a band together in
junior high, a terrible band, but kids used to stand in the
doorway of his garage and listen to us anyway. Bobbing
their heads while his dad's tools rattled on their peg-
board. It was a nice feeling standing up there with people
watching, even if it was just fifth and sixth graders with
animal backpacks and a sheen of candy residue on their
faces. Lisa—as hilarious fate would have it—there among

them.

Tim was in love with her first, and that's probably why we stopped being friends later. She and I used to hear his car start up and pull out onto the street while we sat on her bed, the front bumper scraping every time. There was some anger detectable in the way he hit the gas at the stop sign. He could see my car from his drive-way, parked where he wished his was, and I felt bad about it sometimes. I wished we'd found a way around it.

He died a couple of years after we broke up—after I proposed at a dumpy little inn in Napa and Lisa said no—in a car crash in the fog, rear-ended in his little MG by something much larger that crumpled him like one of the beer cans beside me and kept on going, shedding paint and metal scrapings as if shaking off bug splatter.

At his memorial service, his brother put together a slide show that ran on a loop at the back of the Legion Hall. I remember thinking how orderly his life looked, how it seemed mapped out from day one. Nothing was a surprise, everything went as planned—even the ending, which wasn't true of course. It would have been truer if his brother had shuffled the pictures, let randomness de-fine him so that he was thirty years old one minute and ten the next, screaming on the swings just after throwing his hat in the air at our graduation, standing on the slope of a glacier moments before taking his first steps. That's how most of us live, really, bouncing around our lives like faulty pinballs.

Tim's the one who gave Lisa the Van Morrison al-bum. *Moondance*, for chrissake. I might not forgive him for that.

~

THE MIDDLE GROUND

Sometimes I hear a dog barking through the fog. It's always the same dog; he has a very distinctive bark. It reminds me of a dog I had when I was living with a woman who didn't much care for me, a dog whose bark sounded uncannily like an attempt at speech, like a drunk trying to tell you something important. You'd swear that if you paid a little closer attention you could understand what he was trying to say.

When the dog was in the room, I found myself becoming circumspect, watching what I said. I chose my words carefully around him. When he wasn't there, I tossed them off like baseballs I didn't care if I lost.

". . . never once asked me how *I* . . ."

". . . how am I supposed to . . ."

". . . all that bullshit about waiting for . . ."

". . . *you're* the one . . ."

The girl's voice and the cowboy's float out of the house and hover above me. His voice is, at times, mine, but at other times not. The fog separates the words from their context and they become nearly harmless. They could almost be taken back.

". . . so goddamn sure . . ."

". . . shut up . . ."

". . . always you, never me . . ."

". . . this is pointless . . ."

". . . no shit . . ."

". . . it is . . ."

". . . I know . . ."

There have been other voices too, at other times. The girl has an older sister who got married about a year ago and moved out, and there are the twins next door. Sometimes voices drift over from other houses too, and from the street. I used to think I could collect them and paste them together like a scrapbook, that some hidden meaning would be revealed to me through them. The fog-filled snow globe would shake out and everything would be plain as day. Motives would be clear, judgments would be affirmed, and love would be requited.

". . . I had everything. Now I have nothing . . ."

Go figure.

~

From time to time I'd hear about Lisa. She went on to become something of a celebrity, selling books and DVDs on late night TV and giving motivational lectures in towns around the country where people pronounce theatre "thee-ate-er." I went to hear her once, when she spoke at the community center here. The room was large enough that I could slump in the back without being noticed, though once or twice I caught her squinting in my direction.

The title of her talk was "Moving On"—about how hard it is to get past what you need to get past for the sake of your personal growth, the hurdles you need to vault to become the best you you can be. She described how our past holds onto us like a web, with the bad things tangled up with good things so that it's super tough to cut the threads. She had a PowerPoint and threw out a lot of anecdotes that I recognized from our time together, mixed in with others that must have been either made up or happened with someone else.

I can't imagine her lecture helping anybody with real problems, though she evidently made a decent living at it. A lot of people are desperate for help, is the thing, and they want to believe it's out there somewhere. When someone comes along claiming to have managed what they haven't, and probably never will, they're willing to listen. Once, anyway. I doubt there were many return customers. No one wants that kind of thing rubbed in.

～

The fog—worn through in places and thickened in others with an accretion like scar tissue—obscures and reveals alternately. That's what it has to offer in contrast to unbroken vistas and breathtaking seascapes. If anything is lost, it's the vastness of the night sky and the pinpricks of light that show us how small we are, that put things in perspective. But perspective is nothing more than a trick of the eye, a convergence of lines. It's not music, or memory, or moonlight.

Lisa eventually married an attendee at one of her seminars, a physical therapist from Boise. They had one child, a boy, before the little commuter plane she was taking from a seminar in Reno to a seminar in Turlock disappeared near Lake Tahoe. It took over a year for the wreckage to be discovered, which is hard to believe these days, with GPS and cell phones and the near impossibility of straying from the grid.

A lot of people from here volunteered in the search, skiing cross-country off into the voids that can still be found between highways. I went once myself, back in to a place she and I had skied to when we first started going out, a little valley between two high ridges. A creek ran through the middle of it that we could hear and sometimes see underneath the ice. It was a clear day, I remember, in January or February. A brand new year at a time when we believed in that sort of thing, in scheduled change.

The valley was beautiful and seemed undiscovered to us. We imagined ourselves as pioneers, cutting the first tracks to a new paradise. I don't know why I thought the plane might be there, what exactly seduced me into thinking there might be some symmetry to life, that hers would come back around to me. As it turns out, a pair of backpackers found the pieces of the plane the following summer near Quincy, about a hundred miles off course.

Somewhere between the fifth and sixth beers the cowboy gets in his pickup and drives off. His headlights are swallowed up by the fog, and the sound of his engine fades almost immediately to nothing. Its diminution is not accompanied by the music of Crosby, Sills and Nash. He does not continue out of the frame, windows down and radio cranked, into a future of sloppy gestures and poorly regulated drinking. The girl does not—as fitting as it might be—cry oversalted tears and go on to describe to strangers with exaggerated nostalgia the tortuous course of doomed love.

Instead, the fog ticks onto dry grass and she locks the door and goes to bed.

I finish off number six, hold my hand in front of my face, study it for changes—the broken knuckle straightened, the burn scar healed. Two streets over the familiar dog barks his pidgin, telling me to wait, be patient, all things come in time.

I crumple the last can, flip the dog off, and feed a

vision of Neil Armstrong into a wood chipper.

Toward morning the fog begins to disintegrate, the bottom edge to fray. The window closes so slowly that I don't notice all the things drifting out—hairpins, apricots, snowmelt, deer tracks, phone calls, gas tanks, words words words—I only sense their absence after they're gone, the feeling each of them generated in me lost. I try to call them back, to relearn their hopeless alphabet, but it's impossible. My head is full of broken furniture. There's no more room.

～

I limp as I walk out of the field, my leg gone to sleep. The sidewalk is a gray beach with the fog breaking against it. The road beside me is slick black and shimmering, the centerline glowing like a runway disappearing in promise a hundred yards off. To the east, the mountains are already haloed with the controlled explosions of a new day. I feel the heat gathering behind me and pick up the pace.

Soon, I know, the fog will burn off and everything will be belittled by sunlight. The soft angles and fuzzed lines will harden in the glare. The girl and her cowboy will wake up in separate rooms under the gentle hum of A/C and mistake repetition for renewal. The moon will disappear, then reappear, over and over, and across the wide, featureless valley the last of the lost tribes of Kit Carson will lick their stamps and send their postcards out.

But no one anywhere, not even the dead, will wish they were here.

SILO

OUT BEHIND MY DAD'S HOUSE, just past the edge of the pasture, the federal land begins. It reaches back from there up into the buttes, a cluster of shaved-off hills of volcanic rock covered with thick, brown grass that hover over the house. When the wind blows, which is most of the time, the grass lays over on its side and ripples like an ocean, and the buttes look like big brown breakers bearing down on us. I go over there most weekends and stay with him. He doesn't always remember me, but we get along all right anyway. Sometimes better than when he knew who I was.

"Government stole that land," he says, pointing out the back window at the buttes. "During the war. Sons of bitches."

"Well it's not much good, anyway," I say. "Pretty, but not much use."

"What do you know?" he asks, and he's got a point. I live in town, on a regular street, and there aren't any horses, or cattle, or rice fields anywhere near me. My neighbors are salesmen and engineers and teachers. There's not a farmer in the whole bunch. It's too bad. Sometimes I wish it was all still farm country, that we'd all sit around on someone's porch and watch a storm roll in as though it might make a difference. As it is, we just watch it come and sometimes don't even get out of the way.

One night I opened up my front door to look out at the rain and saw Scotty Browning standing on his lawn in nothing but his shorts. Scotty Browning. A little kid's name, but he's forty-one, same as me. We grew up together, went through school together. We were never close, though. I never really even liked him. Now he lives two doors down, and I don't like him any better.

He used to yell at his wife and his two kids all the time. I could hear him at night even with my doors closed and the TV on. He's got a loud voice that's a little hoarse from being mad for so long, and glass and screen, even the thick stucco of my walls seem to have no effect on it. It's superhuman, like something alien invaders might use to brainwash us over to their side.

I used to pull for Janel, his wife, to just once let loose and give him a little of it back. She never did, though. She just stood there and took it. But there's only so much of that anybody will take, even Janel, and one day while he was at work she packed her things up, put the kids in the car, and left. That night it rained, a mad, driving rain that rattled the downspouts against the side of the house.

It came out of the south, like it usually does, rolling

14

across the buttes in gray ripples, matting the grass up there like dog hair. That's when I looked out and saw him on his front lawn, soaked to the bone, just standing there. I called across to him, to make sure he hadn't been hit by lightning and calcified to a belligerent statue. If that happened, I figured, I'd never be rid of him.

When I called he looked over, but it was as if he was looking at something on the other side of me. Something in the long distance that was maybe promised to him when he was little. His head pivoted as if it wasn't part of him, like a bobble-head doll's. After a minute his eyes settled on me, and he raised his middle finger lazily. Then he turned back toward the buttes and took a drink from a can of beer hanging at his side. It was raining so hard that every once in a while a sheet of it would fall between us and he'd disappear. But when it let up a little, he'd be right there again, staring off at the hills.

"Goddamn Russians," my dad says, sitting up in his La-Z-Boy. "They're the ones put us up to it."

"What?"

"The goddamn missiles. What do you think?"

"There aren't any missiles," I say.

"Bullshit. It's like Swiss cheese up there. They got those silos dug in everywhere, goddamn missiles still in 'em. You think I don't remember?"

His eyes squint up when he talks about it, his pissedoffedness focused for a moment. "Never even bothered to take the shitting things out. Leave us down here with all that radiation leaking down onto us, using us for goddamn guinea pigs. See if our hair'll fall out. Or our nuts'll rot off."

"There's nothing up there," I say, but he doesn't hear

me.

I wonder if he has some kind of Tourette's. A mild version. He never takes off on a full-blown swearing jag the way they're supposed to; it's just kind of a constant, vaguely obscene drone. I don't mind it, really, it's just that he never used to do it. When I was a kid he hardly ever swore. He washed my mouth out once for saying "damn."

"You don't take the Lord's name in vain," he said.

"I didn't," I said. "I just said 'damn.'"

"You're asking for round two."

My sister Carol was watching from the doorway.

"It's only going to give him diarrhea," she said.

Dad turned on her. "You hungry too?" he asked, waving the bar of Dial.

"No thanks. I'm stuffed."

I could feel his arm tense where he held me by the collar.

"You must have got that mouth from the mailman."

I was older than she was, but she was smarter. I wouldn't get the joke, or its meanness, for a couple of years yet. Carol disappeared from the doorway, and a minute later the front door closed.

"That's that," my dad said, letting go of my shirt. "Rinse out."

~

Carol was in love with Scotty Browning's little brother, Bobby. They didn't have any friends of their own, just each other. It was embarrassing for me and Scotty, but they didn't care. They were already talking about getting married. When they were only twelve. When they should have been throwing things at each other. When they should have had nothing in common.

Sometimes they followed me into the hills. They'd walk along behind me when I took my horse up there, holding hands like it wasn't going against nature. Like I said, they should have been natural enemies. They shouldn't have known what they did already, they shouldn't have known about love.

Once in a while Scotty would tag along too. I'd try to get away whenever I saw him coming, but he usually knew where to wait for me so I wouldn't have a chance to turn off. Like an ambush. All of a sudden he'd be standing against a fence post by the trail tossing a rock in the air and smiling crossways at me.

"You and that horse," he'd say, shaking his head. Then he'd fall in beside me.

After a while he'd pick up a stick and beat the grass with it, hoping to scare up some snakes and spook Sonny out from under me. He carried a slingshot, too. For defense, he said. There were wild pigs in the buttes that would sometimes break out on the trail and stare you down for a second before turning and running off into the brush. They'd snarl at you, and you could see their teeth poking up on either side of their mouths. Their eyes were dead like lizards' or snakes' eyes. There were rumors that they'd killed two hunters once, but nobody knew who the hunters were or exactly where it had happened.

There were a lot of stories like that. Like the missile silos. You still hear that one, even now. About how the government laid out this whole string of missile silos in the buttes during the early fifties, during the scare. Deep down, in the bedrock. About how they worked by night, up in the steepest parts, and the flash from their welding torches sparked along the contours. Worked like moles to lay out their vision, a concrete-lined warren hidden beneath the brown grass and the oaks.

They were secret installations, supposedly, a battery of weapons guaranteed to wipe out Russia even if they killed all of us first. They had no defensive purpose, they were designed for pure punishment. The last line of punishment, sneaking up behind the Russians from some nothing hills out on the edge of nowhere just when they thought they were safe—like a Doberman does, not barking, not interested in show, only in effect.

When the government abandoned them, the story goes, they left the missiles in and just covered up the mouths of the silos. The problem was, somebody had lost the map that showed all the locations, and no one could quite remember how many there'd been or where exactly they were. So some were missed and were never sealed up. Until eventually the live oaks and manzanita drew their own cover in over them.

Scotty believed every word of it. He was gullible, but it was more than that. Sometimes he wanted to believe things so badly it was scary. It was like his life depended on this whole string of lies and stories he'd piled together into a ladder of air, and he held onto it like a drowning man.

Bobby laughed at him about it. Carol, though, always tried to explain to him logically how the things he believed couldn't possibly be true. I think he liked being laughed at better. Sometimes Carol would be talking along sensibly and he'd just turn away, glare up the trail toward the high ridge and its lightning-scarred trees as if none of us were there.

"Do you know there are goddamn Russians living right here, right in goddamn town?" my dad asks.

"Sure," I say. "It's different now. They can get out if they want to. Remember they tore the wall down?"

"That was Germany," he says.

"I know. But it was all part of the same thing. They couldn't get out of anywhere. They were all stuck."

"Why do they have to come here?"

"Where else are they gonna go?"

He doesn't answer. He needs these things. They're simple and perfect.

~

One time I was riding Sonny up in the buttes and Scotty fell in beside me out of nowhere.

"What the hell's wrong with them?" he asked, jerking his head toward the trail below us. Carol and Bobby were down there, following a little way behind. They were holding hands and swinging their arms. There was a little grass in my sister's hair from lying beside the trail next to Bobby and looking up at the empty sky. I'd come across them like that once, lying in the grass like they were dead. When I saw them I couldn't help looking up too, to see what it was that held them there so fixed. But there wasn't anything I could see.

"Who knows?" I said.

"Pisses me off."

I climbed off Sonny and let him graze in the long, dry grass beside the trail. Scotty sat in the shade of a live oak and looked down at Carol and Bobby moving toward us.

"Why do they have to come up here?" he said.

"I don't know. Why do you?"

He picked a rock up from beside the trail and tossed it in the air.

"I belong here," he said.

It was probably just bad timing that Bobby and Carol laughed at something right then. Scotty jumped to his feet. He loaded the rock into his slingshot and fired it, hard. It ricocheted off a boulder beside Bobby. He and Carol stopped and gawked up at us, their eyes big and stupid with surprise.

"Hey!" Bobby yelled.

The next one hit him in the foot and he hopped around on the other one for a minute, leaning on Carol's shoulder.

"Cut it out," I said. "Leave 'em alone."

"Fuck you," Scotty said.

The next rock whizzed by Bobby's head. He was almost crying; you could see it even from where we were. Scotty loaded another one in, but they were already turning back so he shot it into the brush off to the side of them.

"Good riddance," he said as we started up the trail again. I looked back once more when we were near the top. They were almost out of sight. They were holding hands again, but their arms weren't swinging and Bobby was limping a little. They looked very small, like toys. Like memories when you catch your mind wandering.

~

"Where's your horse?" my dad says.

"He's gone," I say.

"Good."

When they didn't come back that night, no one was

worried. Everyone figured they'd probably fallen asleep in each other's arms up in the buttes. That's how they were, and it was the natural explanation. It satisfied everyone. It wasn't until late the next day that people started talking about a search party.

They started out around sunset with dogs and flashlights. I went along on Sonny and scouted off to the sides, through the thick brush where you couldn't go on foot. We stayed out the next day too, when most of the others went back and replacements came up to relieve them. It was a big area, with a million places to hide if you wanted to. There were thickets of brush so dense that Sonny just bounced off them, and stands of manzanita that you had to crawl on your belly to get into. The branches twined over you and paths branched off in every direction. You could have taken any one of them and ended up somewhere you'd never been before. Somewhere strange and foreign, where you'd just hear voices, very far away.

No one ever really got used to them being gone, it was just that at some point you had to give up. All of us did eventually, turned around and went back down to the flats, went home. We'd searched for three straight weeks. I don't know what more we could have done.

A couple of nights after the search was called off, my dad set Sonny loose. I was sitting on the couch and I heard his shoes clicking on the blacktop. The hoof beats started off slow, kind of unsure, but by the time he passed our front door he was moving. There wasn't any moon. I couldn't see him as he tore past toward the buttes. All I saw were sparks shooting out from under him, trailing off like little meteorites, until he hit the end of the road and the ground turned to dirt again.

Before long people started saying they'd fallen into one of the silos. Stumbled onto one that had been missed, and the blanket of brush over the mouth had given way beneath them. They fell, down and down, through a darkness thicker than night. But it was soft where they landed—in a stockpile of army overcoats—and they just got up and brushed themselves off. There were C-Rations and water drums down there. That's how they could survive, in an underground city built out of fear and rashness. It was an inevitable explanation for those parts. After a while, with nothing else to go on, it became the truth.

Scotty kept looking. Once, much later, I was up in the buttes and I met him coming down the trail. His clothes were torn from brush snags and there were branches in his hair. I watched him for a minute before he saw me. He was working the trail, walking down it a few steps, then peering off into the brush and calling, quietly, for both of them.

When he looked up and saw me, he puffed out in embarrassment.

"What?" he said.

"Nothing."

"Good answer."

It was still summer up in the buttes. I offered him a drink of water.

"I bet they're watching us right now," he said, wiping the mouth of the bottle on his dirty shirt.

"I doubt it."

"Probably laughing too."

He squinted off into the brush. Then he snorted and shook his head.

"This world's full of idiots," he said.

He had a .22 with him, and he turned and shot into the scrub. I heard the bullet flick through leaves, then thump into the hillside.

"What are you shooting at?" I said.

"Whatever's in there."

He cocked another round into the rifle, and moved past me down the trail.

~

There's a breeze coming through the screen door. I go to close the slider.

"Leave it," my dad says.

"It's gonna rain," I say.

"So what?" he says, leaning back in his chair. "So goddamn what."

I go into the kitchen and get a beer from the refrigerator. It's already starting to rain when I come back into the living room. I stop and stand in the doorway looking out, past my dad in his purple leather chair, at the buttes disappearing under the clouds.

By now it's already been raining for a few minutes over at my house. Down the street, puddles will be forming in the two permanent holes Scotty's feet left in his lawn the time he stood out there all night in the rain. He's probably out there again tonight, glaring off at the buttes. He's like my dad, his anger so focused you wouldn't be surprised to see some kind of killer beam shooting out of his eyes. They're two of a kind. They build their own little worlds, then they don't like what they've made and they want to start over.

My dad doesn't say anything as I wrestle the La-Z-

THE MIDDLE GROUND

Boy through the slider. Even when I bump the footrest
hard against the jamb, he's silent. He doesn't look at me.
Why should he? I'm of no interest. I'm here.

I wheel him out past the porch, through the yard.
The chair's wheels crunch over the fallen fence wires.
Out in the pasture, it's raining hard. The mud grabs at
my shoes. There's an old snubbing post in the middle
where I used to mount up on Sonny. It's rotting out, and
acorn woodpeckers have riddled it with holes. In some of
them you can see the points of acorns sticking out. When
it's windy, like it is now, the wind whistles through the
empty holes. I spin the chair around to face the buttes,
and lean the back of it against the post.

My dad's already soaked. His old chamois shirt clings
to his sunken chest. It lifts weakly when he draws a
wheezing breath, then settles back into its wrinkles. He
blinks against the rain running down into his eyes, but he
still doesn't look at me or say anything when I walk back
across the pasture and into the house.

~

When you're young, you don't think you hold a place in
the world, or that if you left anything would change. But
it does. The whole world collapses around the event, as
if a plug's been pulled. My sister didn't understand that.
She still doesn't.

I read the letter from Mendocino again, awed by its
selfishness. They're expecting their third child. They're
living happily up on the coast, and regret any sorrow or
trouble they might have caused. Which is fine for them,
but for us it doesn't really help much. We're still bogged
down in the same mud, hoping every new storm's the one

24

that will either blow the sky clear or wash us away for good.

I turn on the gas in my father's fireplace, put a couple of logs on for good measure, and throw the letter in. I don't know who I'm protecting or punishing anymore, I just know the letter's got no place here. In the end our lives are a cumulative thing, built out of every turn made or not made.

Say, for instance, you're walking up a hill, following the same old trail like any other day. There's only one way down at that point, back the way you came. But if you keep going past where you usually turn around, past where the path dribbles out into an estuary of animal trails, eventually another view opens up. Another way down. So maybe you keep walking. Across slabs of volcanic rock and bunch grass, over the two rivers, up to the base of the next mountains. By that point, it seems more sensible to just go on. So you do, on across the mountains that turn into row after row of mountains, through stands of timber and barren gullies, until finally you come to the ocean. You walk down to the edge, roll up your pant legs, and let the icy water drag your feet down into the sand. Then you scramble back up the bluff and lie down next to your chosen other. You fall asleep watching the water disappear over the side of the world, and when you wake up maybe the other way back is gone. Maybe the trail home through the hills isn't available anymore.

I take a beach umbrella and a lawn chair out into the pasture and set up next to my dad's chair. The rain's hitting hard on the fabric.

"Damn cloud-seeding Russians," he says.

The two goats come over and try to squeeze under

the umbrella with us. I don't know why they stay in the pasture. Only a few sections of the fence are still standing. There are huge gaps in between where a whole herd of goats could fit through. But they stay put. Not out of laziness, I'm sure, or consideration for us. It's something else. But I have no idea what.

ICE FLOWERS

ANOTHER CALF HAD DIED. IT was Kauffman, his neighbor to the north, who'd found it. The calf had been dead at least a week; there wasn't anything left of use.

"Okay," Wilton said. "I'll make a note of it."

"It's winter. You're aware of that?" Kauffman said.

"I certainly am." Wilton held out his gloved hand to catch a cluster of falling flakes. They melted almost immediately.

Kauffman patted him on the shoulder. "Keep an eye out, Wilt. Things die awful easy."

It was an unnecessary warning to Wilton who, simply by turning ninety degrees to his right, could take in the graves of his wife, his daughter, and both parents on the little birch-tufted hill above the house. Death was a sure thing, yes, but it didn't deserve the level of attention it received. Not in his reckoning.

When he was in fourth grade, he was dragged to five funerals in the span of three months. The Black Summer, he called it. Everyone sweating black stains through their black suits, black curtains on the windows, black fabric draped across the big chair his father slumped into at the end of the day. Wilton didn't keep a single black thing in the house now. At some point—that summer or another like it—the two processes, dying and mourning, had switched places. Death became in his mind the aftermath of grieving; and of sun. So when the Black Summer gave way to the white night of winter, he welcomed it. He watched the snow come from the north, heard a thudding like horses as it broke against the house. On the windows, individual flakes hung briefly in stark outline before falling away. Without thinking, he ran out into it—the first blizzard of the year—with only a shirt and thin shoes, and nearly died. His father found him sitting against the side of the barn, his hands cupped in front of him full of snowflakes.

He held on to them as long as he could, but the heat of the house dulled their edges quickly, blurred their outlines and stole their singularity. Still, he knew there were more where they'd come from. The doctor's announcement that he would lose two toes to frostbite was only of passing concern—there were more where those came from too.

Kauffman's daughter, Flora, waved as Wilton passed along the section of fence that ran closest to their house. She was sitting on the porch with a book in her lap, content as could be even with the snow coming heavier and filling in the folds of the blanket draped across her legs. The influenza that had taken his wife and daughter had almost taken her, too. She'd been weakened by it, Kauffman said. Had to quit her job in the city and come home to recover. Wilton didn't know how it could possibly be healing, sitting out like that in all weather.

He lifted his hand to wave back, then let it fall again. She wasn't looking at him anymore; she was gazing up into the falling snow. When she stuck out her tongue to catch a snowflake, he looked away in embarrassment. He was familiar with the taste—it was nothing, or nearly nothing.

He herded the remaining cattle into the barn and pushed a hay bale out of the loft. He wasn't much of a farmer, never had been, but you inherited most of your life, like it or not. The part you could decide for yourself was a small wedge you had to pull aside from the larger pie and save for later.

He kept his camera room at the outside temperature to prevent, or at least to slow, the ice crystals' clumping impulse. Isolating them was tricky. They tended to be drawn to one another, to stick and blend at the slightest urging. His breath condensed around him as he set the apparatus up and moved a slide into position under the hopper. Lifting the release lever, he let a fine dusting of snow shower onto the glass. It looked like nothing at this stage—jagged white motes. He swung the camera into position, the lens set at the ideal focus, and tripped the shutter. There was a whirring click that disturbed nothing, the blink of an eye. Then quiet again as he slid another plate into position.

The darkroom, in contrast, had to be kept warm or

the chemicals wouldn't work properly. He tried to avoid the intrusive analogy to birth—the musty darkness, the images manifesting before his eyes—as the ice flowers bloomed, their petals and spines slightly distorted by the shallow layer of developer. Each sheet contained an orderly array of unique geometry he was the first to see. One by one, he hung them up to dry, then heated up a small pot of stew and sat down to his solitary dinner.

Was he lonely? He may have been at one time. But if so, he'd outlived it. If there was any remnant, it was only the trace hunger you feel when you stop yourself from eating your fill. The void is taken up soon enough by something else, and the next time you find you need even less.

In the middle of December, about a week before Christmas, it stopped snowing. The air turned still and cold, the sky went a naked blue. At night, the stars drifted slowly overhead like river ice breaking apart. Wilton found it easy to collect his crystals at first, sliding the top layer from drifts close to the house as if skimming cream. Soon, though, the crystals grew stale, losing their personality. Points drooped, edges dulled. He found himself having to go deeper and deeper into the woods to find good specimens.

There, he would shake a small tree by the trunk and catch the flakes on a panel of sheet metal. The sun glanced off them, lighting the facets like broken glass showering from the dome of heaven. He laughed, tried to think where in the world he'd gotten that—one of his mother's school primers, he suspected. The high-flown language she loved, so unsuited to their rough-cut lives. It occurred to him that Flora might have come across the line in one of her books. On his way in from collecting, he stopped at the fence.

"Are you familiar with 'the dome of heaven'?"

She finished the sentence she was in the middle of, then looked up. Other than an occasional muttered greeting, it was the first real thing he'd ever said to her.

"I encounter it every day with wonder," she said.

Her beatific smile unsettled him, and her answer was singularly unhelpful. He considered explaining his question a little more, telling her what had brought it on. But it would take too long, and the crystals in his collection case would suffer. He felt her watching him as he turned away; it put an odd hitch in his stride, he had no idea why—he'd been walking, after all, for years.

The thaw came in the early morning, with colder air close behind. Even deep in the woods, the snow melted and refroze, the crystals merging into hard communities of ice. He walked farther than he could remember having done before—even when he was a boy and would walk all day in a single direction, straight out across the plains or through the woods until the sun passed its zenith and he had to turn around again. His strides were longer now, he assumed; that was how he managed to pass out of his known territory on a day that was shorter than almost any other day of the year.

Fat drops of melt rained down on him from the trees; the snow underfoot was heavy and clung like mud to his boots. Here and there a smaller tree was bent nearly over, weighted down by the high water content. He came across a rabbit's trail, and followed it to where the tracks ended in the middle of a clearing. There were no burrows in the snow, no limbs to jump to, no sign of any back-tracking. The tracks simply stopped. A hawk was the likeliest explanation, if not the most satisfying. Wilton preferred to believe that the rabbit had found its way out somehow, back to the safety of the trees. One mad jump. The closest tree was twenty feet away.

The terrain became steeper. He climbed a ridge and followed its spine northwest toward where he could see a narrow plume rising. Someone burning slash, maybe, but he was well beyond even the farthest outlying farms. When the trees abruptly ended at the crown of the ridge, he saw the source—a hot spring tucked into a little notch in the hill. The steam was thick above the water, but thinned out periodically as a gust of wind drew it aside like a curtain. It was during one of these partings that he saw Flora stand up in the center of the pool.

He could see the lines of her body clearly—her breasts, pale and narrow, her waist too thin above her cocked hip. One side of her ribs seemed to be partly sunken in, an indentation he took to be a scar of some kind. She spun slowly with her arms out, setting the steam into a whirl around her, a benign tornado.

There was a beauty to the sight that troubled him, knowing it wasn't meant for him. Still, he didn't look away. At one point, as the cloud of steam began to close around her again, she leaned her head to the side and wrung her hair out gently. In that movement, worlds seemed to be undone. He'd seen something like it, he thought, in a book; his wife's *Golden Bough*, maybe.

He was just at the edge of the trees, mostly hidden, but some movement drew her attention—his shifting from one foot to another, or a branch behind him shedding its load of snow. She wrapped her arms across her chest and dropped quickly into the pool. She had to emerge part way again to retrieve her dress, but Wilton had already turned away and started back by then.

Somehow he wandered twice from his trail, and had to range some way out before cutting it again. She was on her porch when he emerged onto his land. Steam was rising from her hair and her eyes were closed. He tried to pass silently, crossing to the far side of the narrow field.

"How was your walk?" she called across the muddy fringe of her father's pasture.

"Fine."

"Was it good both going and coming back?"

She said it with a wide smile, and afterward laughed with her face half-hidden behind her book. He thought she was laughing at him. He felt his face flush, and turned back toward his house. She called after him—"I'm sorry!"—but he kept walking, his feet stomping harder through the crust.

Lying in bed he tried, as he did every night, to recall his wife and daughter. And again, as every other night, he failed. He could call to mind a sweeping variety of ice crystals, thousands of them, but he couldn't call back the familiar lines of their faces. He had only the one picture—the two of them together in a clearing somewhere, Elizabeth looking tired, and Dahlia beside her with the face of an old pioneer woman. They had aged so quickly, in no time at all. Then they were gone.

Perhaps it was this failing of his memory—which he

took for a deeper failing—that had made him initiate, on his weekly trip into town, a catalog of faces. They were objectively different, nearly as divergent as ice crystals, but the indexing criteria were immensely harder to isolate. Where a crystal might be stelliform or palmate, plated, prismatic, dendritic, a face was . . . what? Something more than its relative shape or size, its beauty or homeliness. There was a component he couldn't quite define. How a certain face could trigger a specific reaction in the viewer—distrust, happiness, anger—for no reason that he could name. His notebook entries were, even to him, cryptic and unhelpful:

Oval, eyes bluish shot with green, indifferent symmetry.

Animate block, deliberately obfuscate.

Dinner plate, blank, stained with scraps of last meal.

Belligerent nose, alcohol veined, judgmental chin with arrogant stubble.

He abandoned the project quickly. What was the point, really? None of it brought him any closer to understanding why some people stayed and others vanished.

~

Over the next days he worked harder and longer than usual, feeling an unexpected urgency. He photographed and developed nearly two dozen plates, working well past dark in the closeness of his darkroom. The onset of an ice storm outside hardly drew his attention. He heard pellets rapping against the side of the house and on the windowpanes in the kitchen. At one point, a loud cracking came from the north, from the direction of Kauffman's. A tree branch succumbing, he assumed. There'd be work in the morning, wood to cut and clear. He'd help Kauffman, who always helped him, though he didn't have the time for it.

A commotion woke him early—Kauffman yelling, wood splintering. He watched out the window as a pair of horses dragged the fallen porch roof away from the house and Henning, the fire department chief, pulled Flora out with the help of a younger man he didn't recognize. They set her on a wide plank and loaded her into the back of a flatbed. Her hair hung out over the tailgate as the truck moved slowly through the snow. He saw Kauffman looking across at him, and backed away from the window.

A professor at the university had been pestering him for the last year about collecting his images into a manuscript. He told Wilton there was a great demand for it among meteorologists, physicists, even mathematicians. He could fill a gap in their knowledge, the professor said. So Wilton spent the rest of the day collating his prints, indexing them to his personal taxonomy. He wrote a short introduction in the last of the daylight, a paragraph full of excesses he thought Flora might have nodded her head over and smiled at:

The careful observation of the crystals' felicitous structure reveals a far more elegant design than the naked eye could have alone imagined. Held in the hand, they are small and transitory, but here on film they bloom to their full grandeur. Gaze upon their multiform grace in awe—for their beauty not only illustrates the cold calculus of determinate nature, it expresses in exquisite form the history of their journey through the clouds to us. Who has not followed in his heart as they seem in a wind to rise even as they fall, and to flower at the advent of spring only in melting?

In addition to his wife and daughter, he tried that night to call Flora back. She eluded him likewise. She should have been fresh in his mind, but there was only a kind of glow, a faint heat like the sun through drifting snow. He thought of her coming out of the water, her body steaming, the lines of her vibrating in the cold. She was looking at him, but she couldn't see him. She leaned her head back and studied with some concern a stray cloud about to pass in front of the sun. When it did, Wilton knew, the world would turn again to ice.

He didn't collect any crystals for a while. There wasn't much point; everything was slick and frozen, useless. One afternoon, three or four days after the storm, he found himself by his north fence. He hadn't planned it, and the discovery surprised and unsettled him. It was something that happened to old men.

The fence was still half-buried. He stepped over it and crossed the edge of Kauffman's pasture. The porch roof had been hauled off to the side and broken up for firewood. Her chair was on its side by the corner of the house. It was frozen in, and it took some doing to free it. He set it on the porch and leaned it back the way she liked to sit, tipped on its hind legs.

"Don't blame yourself," Kauffman said from behind him. "I don't."

"No," Wilton said, turning.

"Even if you heard it."

"I thought it was a branch."

Kauffman studied him. "You didn't go look, though."

"It happens all the time. You know."

Kauffman hadn't shaved lately, and he seemed to be leaning slightly, as if a wind were blowing from his side.

"I don't know if she suffered," he said.

"She never seemed to."

"I mean, when it happened."

Wilton thought about that, unsure how to judge it. He wanted to say something helpful.

"Like you said, things die easily."

The blow came quickly; he had no time to react. Kauffman stood over him, huffing. The look on his face held too many components to isolate. He was howling, a kind of wail like something caught; his teeth were grinding, his eyes pressed shut so that the thin, white lids were almost transparent. Wilton sat up where he'd fallen and watched the blood from his nose run in a stream into the snow. He didn't resent the punch, or the wailing, or any of it. He himself had seen Flora nearly every day, counted on it, and he found it difficult now too reconciling himself to her absence.

〜

His original title for the book, *A Pictorial Study of Ice Flowers*, was changed by the publisher to *Ice Crystals*. Simple and straightforward, qualities Wilton would have admired at one time. He couldn't put his finger on when that had changed. The truth was, the book didn't interest him much once it was done. It became history, which he had little use for. He continued to collect and to catalog his findings in a kind of revolt against its finality. There would be subsequent editions, amendments and supplements presenting themselves, conceivably forever. He looked forward to the job's futility, its Sisyphean labor. Besides, what else was he to do with his remaining time?

He had discovered, on later visits, that the crystals

around the hot spring were markedly different from those found elsewhere. There was an extravagance to them—intricate filigree between the arms, stunning prismatics, stars within stars. Late in the season he made one last trip out there, collecting close to the water's edge along the demarcation between ice and snow. He carried a loupe with him to get a preliminary idea of the crystals' form. They were some of the finest of his long, eccentric career. He knew that was how others viewed his coming and going, but it had never bothered hm. It was a life with a purpose, wasn't it?

The first hard flakes that overtook him on his way back from the spring were sharp and graceless, streaking nearly horizontal. They stung his neck, pelted against his legs. Deeper into the woods, though, the wind died and the snow grew thicker and softer. There was a kind of music to it he'd always been only half-conscious of— the tick of weighted branches, the sigh like waves washing between the trees, rising and falling with the muffled voice of a distant conversation. He sat down to listen with his back against a birch tree.

DOUBLE HELIX

HIS LITTLE GIRL FLAPPED HER vestigial arms and Ernie felt his love swell and swell like an overfed fuel line—what if it burst now, with Daisy so helpless and, except for him, alone?

After dark, he carried her over the fence to the shuttered pool where they floated together in the reflected stars. She flicked her armlets and sped in circles around a satellite tracking slowly across the deep end. A car passed with its bass thumping, shock waves rippled in harmony across the pool, warping the night sky.

Was it worth it, someone had asked—who, he couldn't remember, no friend surely—the trips, the substitute existence, the fuck-all attention to reality? Wrong question, he'd said. How much love is too much?—that was the real question.

No one could agree, anyway, on the damage. How

39

much was lasting. Maybe it wasn't his fault, maybe his chromosomes were just fine and not shredded, as hysterics claimed, by lysergic razors. Processed food, tainted water—the air itself might have conspired against them. What good was guilt, in any case. What comfort was that to Daisy?

She waggled her web-strung feet and sped across the water.

"How are you going to explain it to her?" Cynthia had asked, some time before the door slammed. "When she's old enough."

"What's old enough?"

He hadn't meant to be difficult, or a smartass. It was a legitimate question. How old did a child have to be to benefit from the knowledge that her parents had played so carelessly with the future?

Every summer, as soon as school let out, they made the drive over the mountains to the ocean. Daisy would sit up and begin giggling as they crossed the last ridge and the first ragged wisps of coastal fog swept past the car. She held her fingerless hand on the window and watched as the condensation formed a mitten around it. Then the ocean, and the sun crashing down, caroming off the waves.

She scooted across the sand on her belly toward the water. He couldn't help her, she wouldn't allow it. He walked beside her, his simian tracks unseemly alongside the sleek lines spooling out behind her.

The world came to her, it was true. A sea otter first, then a pod of dolphins. They nudged her toward deeper water. He could hear her giggling, the fins circling her like the ribs of a playpen. A ray leapt over in a high arc. People watched, mouths open. He stood waist-deep in cold water, her laughter rising and falling, washing in to him on the onshore breeze.

"The fuck is wrong with you?" Running past him, board slapping the water. Daisy protesting in trills. How could he explain, their worlds intersecting only tangentially? He was cited for child endangerment.

Daisy watched the shoreline recede, the fog close over. All this is real, he promised her on their way back across the mountains. All of it. The land melting away behind them, the whistle of the gulls circling around inside the car like the echo of a judgment uttered so quietly and so long ago it could hardly have been true.

COAST STARLIGHT

CLIFFORD COULD HAVE BEEN ANYONE, though no one from around Corning. He was too easy in his skin, standing with his hands loose at his sides, the first person in years to pay any attention to the PLEASE WAIT TO BE SEATED sign. He rocked a little on his feet, his thin legs bowing out at the knees. When he flipped up his clip-on sunglasses, his pupils floated like drops of ink in milky green irises, neglected looking things. If she'd been a little younger she might have blushed, but she'd long since stopped being embarrassed or flattered by men's stares. Her beauty was something she'd had to acknowledge early on, even if she couldn't appreciate it herself.

He slid into the middle booth and ordered scrambled eggs, then smothered them in Tabasco. Sweat broke out across his face as he ate. He went through almost half a canister of napkins, which she'd have to refill after he was gone. She watched the sweat drip onto the table and bead up on the film of oil that never scrubbed all the way off.

Afterward, at the register, he pushed a card across the counter.

"I know this sounds like a line," he said. "But I'd like to put you in the movies."

It did sound like a line, as a matter of fact.

"What kind of movies are these?"

"The real kind," he said. "Not what you're thinking."

"I'm not thinking anything."

"Even better."

She finished her shift and the sun went down while he sat out in the parking lot in his Lincoln with the radio on. Her boss asked if she wanted him to walk her out to her car, but she said no, it was okay. He wasn't dangerous. She could tell.

In a way, she was right.

~

It was the implication in her daughter's question, the way she asked it as she herself might have asked her own mother, that made her start thinking about Clifford again: "Don't you wish something exciting would happen to you, just once?"

Her life, in other words, was a pitiful thing, hardly worth keeping track of. And yet something had happened—or nearly happened—something that could have been put down to a little girl's fantasy, sitting in her room on the blunt edge of nowhere cutting pictures out of magazines, if she'd been that kind of little girl. But she'd always been able to see the eventual disappointment hidden in fantasies, just as she could see the inevitable fading of her own looks when she stood in front of the mirror.

She'd been going out with Matias for a couple of months by then. In his mind it was serious, if not necessarily in hers. It was possible she'd love him some day, she didn't know. For now he was a wall, and that's what she needed. Solid and unmoving, with a fine scar running along the edge of his chin where he'd cut himself with a grape knife when he was a kid. No one bothered her when she was with him, even the older men steered clear. He wasn't mean like the other boys—calling girls *putas* and bitches—he had a soft streak in him. It would likely get ground down eventually, but there might be a livable spell until then. They might have ten good years, maybe more.

He was afraid of her beauty, as many people seemed to be. He touched her like he was defusing a bomb. She could feel him shaking against her that night, this big man with thick, work-scarred fingers. When he tried to put his hand under her bra, she let him. It was a small concession that didn't cost her much. He almost cried at her generosity. She stroked his hair like a child and watched an owl at the end of the orchard row dive in a sudden burst to snatch up a mouse. She thought about Clifford, imagined the owl was him, his skinny frame swooping among the trees. Matias bit her nipple and she let out a little chirp, then shifted in the bucket seat in a futile effort to get comfortable.

The next day Clifford was back, this time ignoring the PLEASE WAIT TO BE SEATED sign like everyone else. He looked a little healthier, his eyes less muddy. Every now and then he tapped something into an electronic organizer. It was an exotic thing in those days—more for effect than practical use, Elena thought—separating him from the common people the way a cravat or a cane might have twenty years earlier.

"You didn't call," he said.

"Of course not."

"I'm serious about this. You can check me out with the trades, I'm legit."

She had no idea what the trades were, but didn't say so. It was another part of his show, a private language to impress her.

"Do you know where you are?" she said.

"More or less."

"We raise olives here, and dust. That's it."

"You're beautiful."

"Don't talk to me like that, please."

He ordered French toast this time, and wolfed it down. He didn't linger as long in the booth, but he left another identical card under the edge of his plate. On the back he'd written: *You put them all to shame.*

She still had the card. The edges had started to separate, one corner bent like a pig's ear. She laughed at the fact that she lived in such a place and in such a way that a pig's ear was the first comparison to present itself. That was part of the problem: she couldn't see herself anywhere but where she was. She never imagined other towns, a different life. When she looked out the window she saw olive trees, rice fields, and the stumpy tanks of the cement plant. The world did not curve out beyond the edge of her vision into rain forests and deserts and kingdoms, it butted up against the dry hills and stopped there.

It was unusual, then, when that night she dreamed of just that, another life, a life in which she felt eyes lingering on her without wanting to hide. She teased and laughed and knew that later on she would be with a man she'd just met, looking out through plate glass windows onto waves and gulls, wrapped in sheets so soft they whispered against her skin like crickets. They would talk in the cryptically mutual way that people in love, real love, talked, understanding everything with a minimum of effort. Wine would follow dinner followed by wine.

She woke in a near panic and showered hurriedly, afraid to touch herself. She drove straight to work, no detours past the park and the duck ponds, no singing to herself under the radio. She was afraid the memory of the dream would persist in those favorable surroundings, rather than dissolving in the sun slanting through the windshield. Still the thought kept creeping back: What if she was beautiful not just here, but everywhere? What if she left this place and people still watched her; what if they saw something in her—like Clifford did—something that could be shared without giving herself away?

It wasn't until her eyes had adjusted that she noticed Matias in the booth where Clifford would have been, his arms tucked in at his sides and his head ducked down the way he did to make himself smaller. He always worried he'd frighten her away. But she wasn't a bird or a squirrel or some other tender thing. When he got down on a knee and a gray puff of cement dust lifted from his jeans, the restaurant tunneled toward her, the sounds of the freeway and the clatter of dishes rose to an aching pitch as if someone had thrown the volume knob all the way over.

She fell back into herself with a crash.

In a way, it was a relief, though she had a headache later and had to spend her break in the bathroom with a Coke and a couple of Ibuprofens. Her eyes ached with a pressure like the heel of a hand pushing down. From the fall, was how she put it to herself. As if it was something physical that had happened to her, a wrong step on the ice, or a ladder going out from under her.

When Clifford showed up the next time, Elena and Matias were married and Carla was almost a year old. Matias had done well; he was good to her and she didn't have any regrets. Very few. She could have done without the cement dust he carried everywhere with him—in the creases of his shirts, on the soles of his shoes, in the gaps in his thinning hair. After the rare rains that came like drunk rages out of the north, she'd find clots of hardened cement cast off around the house and through the yard. Sometimes there were full boot prints, big and ungainly, strung around the fence line where he paced on his sleep-less nights like a guard.

"I'm afraid you won't be here when I wake up," he'd said once to explain it.

"Where would I go?"

He should have smiled then, it would have been enough. But instead his face went cloudy and tight thinking about all the places she could go if she wanted to. A map of the world scrolled across his vision, each road perfectly capable of taking her away from him.

~

Clifford stood with his hands on his hips, sporting a scraggly beard now and wide, black-rimmed glasses riding halfway down his nose. Even before his car came flying across the overpass, something had made her look up, something like a sound but not quite. It reached her ahead of the Lincoln, preceding the car as though it had created the car rather than the other way around.

He'd developed a faint limp that she only noticed as he made his way down the aisle to his booth. More acting, she thought, but then decided—no, something had shifted in him. He moved more deliberately, more seriously somehow, not the cocky careless way he had before. It embarrassed her that she was happy to see him. He made her feel wanted in a way she wasn't used to.

"Welcome back," she said. "Eggs?"

"Just toast and coffee."

As she poured, he held up a sheaf of thumbed pages held together with brads, red lines and notations in the margins.

"Your movie," he said.

Sure enough, there was her name centered on the page in capital letters: ELENA.

"Is it a tragedy?" She tried to laugh, but it came out too loud and a little crooked.

"Is your life a tragedy?"

"No. A comedy, more like."

"Same thing, different scenery."

She only had one other table, a couple of pressers from the olive oil plant, their fingers and palms stained black. They hid them under the table when she took their order. Then they took turns in the bathroom trying to scrub them clean, but it didn't make much difference. Shelly, who cleaned the bathrooms after closing, complained constantly about the stains in the sinks she couldn't get out, the oil slicks on the counters. Elena passed by Clifford's table again after bringing their orders out.

"Why is it my movie?" she said.

"I had it written for you. I described you to this writer friend of mine, I painted a picture in his head. I'm pretty good at that."

"I see."

"Not just the way you look, though, your—" outlining with his hands the shape of her, "but the way you carry yourself. Like there's another you hidden inside, the same way you're holed away in this little town here. No offense."

"Is that what the movie's about?"

"It's an allegory. An action allegory."

"Meaning?"

"It's a story that tells another story."

"With shooting, etcetera."

"Yes. Some shooting, etcetera."

He had a new card. She pulled it out from under the saucer as she watched him get in his car and drive back across the overpass. Dark letters slanting across the top of the card announcing what she guessed was the movie's title: *Out From The Shadows*.

~

The late sun through the kitchen window lit up the ever-present dust, shivering and dancing like a swarm of insects. The chicken mole crunched faintly as she chewed. Everything—not just in her house, but throughout the town—was coated with it, cement dust and field dust, dust stirred by tires and feet and the wind. The houses and stores and the two churches huddled inside a perpetual cloud.

"How far have you ever been?" she asked Matias, slumped like a question mark over his plate, half asleep. He was working twelve hour shifts now. Advancement had its drawbacks as well as its perks.

"How far what? What do you mean?"

"I mean away from here."

He thought and chewed. She could see the gray coating on his nose hairs as he breathed in and out.

"Fresno, I guess. When I was a kid, for 4H."

"I haven't been out of Corning once. Did you know that?"

"Well Fresno wasn't much. You're not missing anything."

"I'd hate to think that. If I thought there wasn't anything worth seeing outside of here, I'd drown myself in the bathtub."

Carla made a noise like a lawnmower refusing to start, and Elena laid her hand softly on top of her head. Her hair was so thin and fine, not like Elena's. She could feel the heat rising up into her hand, skin on skin transferring.

"I'd like to see some of it. Someplace else."

Matias winced as a grain of cement wedged into a crack in his back tooth. He took a long drink of water and waited for the pain to subside.

"Like where?" he said.

"I don't know. L.A. maybe."

"Los Angeles?"

"Yes, Los Angeles. L.A."

"What, like Disneyland?"

"No. I don't know, maybe. Carla might like that. But other things too—museums, the ocean, movie studios."

"I don't know. We don't know anybody."

She wasn't sure how much he knew about Clifford. Not that she was hiding anything, really.

"This is our chance, while Carla's still little. Before she starts school."

"That's a long way off still."

"Not that far."

He leaned back and smiled across at her. "There's no hurry."

The smile infuriated her, the same smile she'd seen all her life—a smile of tolerance, thinking her beauty was an advantage with no downside.

She drank a bottle of wine by herself after Matias and Carla had gone to bed, something she never did. It was a pitiful rebellion. The determination and confidence she felt as she stood naked in front of the bathroom mirror didn't last—it was just a body, nothing more, something she wasn't even responsible for.

She had to call in sick the next day, another thing she never did. She didn't know if Clifford came in or not; she never asked anyone, and nobody mentioned him to her.

~

She called the number on the card twice from the pay phone by the bathrooms, and hung up both times. What would she say? What was she willing to do? That seemed to be the question.

It's possible to go through life without answering those kinds of questions, and Elena tried. She thought she could starve them out, that by refusing to answer them she could banish them, but they filtered in through the windows and doors with the dust, swirled up around her as she moved through the house or wheeled Carla in her stroller to the playground. They became part of the flavor of everything, along with all the other contaminants.

She left a note for Matias finally, said she was going to see the ocean—which was partly true. She took Carla to her mother's. She wouldn't be gone long, she said, three days at the most.

"It's an affair, isn't it?" her mother said, twice. She was excited by the idea, even gave Elena tips for making it memorable.

"Leave him wanting more," she said, pouring a mini bottle of screw-top champagne into their orange juice. She lifted Carla's little hand to wave goodbye through the screen door when Elena left for the train station, her face flushed and her eye squinted in a suggestive wink. Elena had never seen her so proud; it was an unhappy discovery.

There was hardly any shade on the platform. She huddled under the narrow awning with an older woman who smiled but didn't say anything, a paper bag at her feet bulging with neatly folded clothes. How much would Elena have if she packed up and left, she wondered. Not much more than that, if it was down to essentials.

She found a seat by a window and watched the sun drop behind the hills. It disappeared quickly, and then the valley became very dark. Here and there the lights of a plant or a county prison flicked past. The towns got bigger as she headed south, then smaller again past San Jose. Even the smallest looked welcoming in the dark, ribbons of light strung out along invisible streets and up rivers and creeks that would be almost dry now.

The name of the train, printed at the top of the ticket, was the "Coast Starlight." She liked the sound of it, as if the stars along the coast were somehow different from the ones she saw at home, brighter and more fixed, looking directly down on her. She liked that they named the train. She didn't know they did that. It made the whole trip seem more exalted somehow, a forged path through fields of clamoring starlight.

At one point she fell asleep, and when she woke up two girls about her age were sitting across the aisle. They were dressed in smooth silk tops unbuttoned partway down. One of them dangled her high heel from her toes, bobbing it up and down to a song in her head. The girls ignored their surroundings thoroughly, only glancing once or twice derisively out the window.

"Jesus Christ," one of them said. "Where the hell are we?"

The man in the seat in front of them turned and helpfully told them the name of the town they were passing through. They smiled, then rolled their eyes when he wasn't looking.

"Like it matters," one whispered.

Elena fell asleep again, and when she woke up the next time the train was pulling into a large station with arched doorways and a tile roof. Lights blazed out the windows and she could see streets leading off brightly into the distance. She stood up and leaned close to the window.

"Where are you going?" one of the girls asked. The girls were glamorous and made Elena feel shabby in her print dress and flats.

"Los Angeles," she said.

"Ooh. Good for you."

"You'd better hurry then," the other said. She was tall and thin with a nose that seemed a little too small for her face. "They won't turn the train around."

"What? Is this it?"

"That's Sunset Boulevard right over there. Those lights."

"Oh god, thanks!" She hefted her overnight bag and tucked the little box of snacks under her arm. As the train pulled away, the two girls waved through the window. She waved back. Her heart was thumping and she could feel the heat from the pavement rising up to her. Inside the station, she found a pay phone and fished Clifford's card out of her bag. He'd be surprised, no question. What would he say? She realized she hadn't planned any farther than this moment, past the phone call.

She dropped her money in, and a voice told her to deposit more. She looked at the paper tag above the receiver, saw it was a different area code from the one she was dialing. As she dug for more change down through the stubby eye pencils and half-empty powder tubs, the tarnished necklace and the pair of cracked turquoise earrings, an unpleasant revelation dawned on her. She should have known, of course: most girls she met behaved as if life were a race and Elena had been given a head start. She stepped out of the booth, walked back through the station doors and looked up at the sign—SANTA BARBARA—dangling from the eaves.

She had a little money left after paying for a return ticket, so she bought herself an ice cream cone. It was a silly, extravagant thing. She didn't even like ice cream much. But this was the closest she would ever get to being somebody else, so she did what *she* might have done. While she licked the drips from her hand, she laughed quietly at the idea of showing up at Clifford's door unannounced, standing on his doorstep with her little flower-weave bag in her hand. His reluctant courtesy as he invited her in. And instead of anger, she felt an unwanted kinship with the two girls on the train, who were probably still laughing, leaning their glittering heads against each other in the passing lights. Maybe they were masquerading too, seeing what it felt like to wield a little power.

She thought she could smell the ocean, a briny smell like sweat. She didn't know, she'd never been close enough before; maybe it was just the station, all the bodies passing through. The night was clear and there were stars littered out to the horizon. They were a little brighter, maybe, but other than that no different from the ones she knew at home. It wasn't disappointing, exactly—it seemed, in fact, about what she was due. She'd lied to get here, to herself most of all. If there were sins, as she'd always been told, that had to be one.

~

"I was hoping you'd aged badly," Clifford said some years later, the last time he came through. Elena poured his coffee while he dragged his finger through the sheen of oil on the table.

"Was there ever a movie? Or did you get those cards printed somewhere around here."

"There was a movie." He tapped his temple. "It was a

beautiful thing, breathtaking. In meetings—when I described it—all these jaded Hollywood guys sat up in their chairs, hanging on every word. I had a picture of you I'd taken you didn't know about. I had it printed twenty by thirty and sat it on an easel while I talked. They saw you like I did, saw the camera hang on every move you made, never wanting to leave you."

"So what happened?"

Clifford shrugged, a slow slump that rippled through the baggy shoulders of his blazer.

"They couldn't get a star to sign on. For the guy."

"Oh."

"They were afraid of you, Elena. That's what it was. They were afraid all the light and the power and the love would turn toward you."

She doubted that, but she didn't mind him saying it.

"I started down there once, you know," she said.

"You did? When?"

"A while ago. When I was younger."

"What happened?"

"I turned around."

He smiled, leaning down to meet his cup halfway. "Probably just as well."

"You think so?"

"I don't know. But that's what you say, right?"

She nodded, but it wasn't. Not to herself, anyway. In the privacy and security of her own head, she finished the trip. She sat out on his patio with him and let the sun—softened by the ocean—drape itself over her. They drank some kind of cocktail his housekeeper made, but she didn't get drunk. She never lost her head, just took it all in. She avoided looking in the housekeeper's face to prevent herself from seeing her or her mother there, and sipped from the glass that never seemed to empty as the stars began appearing one by one, out of the haze hanging between her and the ocean, cool fires burning outside the drag of time. Ice clinked in their glasses as they discussed the shooting schedule for the next day.

She always stopped there, before the story became ridiculous, before the probable reality intruded—Clifford's apartment a drab warren on some nondescript street, the sky sooty and gray, sirens and drunken quarrels drowning out the distant waves. The ending wasn't important anyway, it wasn't even an ending necessarily. What passed for an ending could easily be just a gap between two halves. An intermission. There wasn't any sure ending until you were dead, and then it hardly mattered how you got there. That's how she put it to herself, anyway, on the days she let her mind off its leash.

At the end of her shift, she sat at the counter next to Shelly, who was flipping through a *National Enquirer*, tsking and shaking her head.

"These people got everything you could want, and nine times out of ten they piss it away," she said.

"You think it's different here?"

"Jesus yes. Are you kidding? Nobody's got anything *to* piss away."

Elena watched the famous faces flip by—smiling, angry, surprised—stars with their dogs, with their children, newly minted couples looking like they never expected to meet an obstacle where they lived. Maybe one of these days there'd be a picture of Clifford, dapper and successful, with his latest discovery, a girl something like her.

She shooed him out of her mind and thought instead about Matias waiting for her when she got off the train, Carla curled into his shoulder. How he managed a thin smile and walked with her back to the truck without ever asking one question. She'd taken it as an act of kindness at the time, and was grateful to him. But in the years since she'd considered whether it might not have been just a lack of curiosity, that maybe he was like everyone else after all—wanting above anything to know just what he knew, and nothing more.

The last of the light was long gone from the sky when she closed out. There might have been stars, but she couldn't see anything past the reflections in the windows. In the carousel by the register there was a slice of pie that had been there as long as she could remember, cherry she thought. She tapped the glass case and a cloud of gray dust rose up, swirled around, and settled like powdered light on the crust.

LAKE MARY JANE

HER LEG HURT WORSE NOW, a day after the alligator rose out of the murk and clamped onto it, and everything was so much more complicated. When the gator had bit down, it was just a thing that was happening to her. Not a pleasant thing, sure, but simple. Now people she'd never met were picking it apart, like the expert on the emergency room TV saying "A ten-year-old girl? There's no way. If the alligator wanted to take her, there's nothing she could have done about it."

"I should have saved her," her dad said, yanking the plug on the TV.

"She saved herself," Emily said. "That's even better."

Anna thought about that, and wasn't so sure. She'd pulled as hard as she could on the jaws, yes, but when the alligator had released her he did it without much fuss, almost gently. And when she collapsed on shore she could see his knobby head a little ways out watching her out of one eye. The lid had blinked twice, like a private code, before he sank under again.

～

"People are skeptical," the reporter was saying, one side of his mouth smiling. "You understand."

Before he showed up, they'd all been sitting close together on the couch with the air conditioner humming and the TV on quiet. A nature show about red pandas.

"No, I don't understand," her dad said. "Are you calling her a liar? A child who just had her leg torn up by a fucking alligator?"

"Come on, what really happened?"

Her dad's temper surprised her sometimes—when he got mad at her for spilling a glass or knocking something over—but he always apologized. In the hug afterward, she could feel love up and down his arms, every hair holding onto her.

"It doesn't matter, dad."

She was limping a little, and the medicine was making her sleepy. Her dad reached behind him and pushed her back, out of the doorway. When she fell, the reporter pointed at her on the floor:

"Get that," he said to a man with a camera.

It surprised her a little, the sound of her dad's punch, how it was soft and hard at the same time. Not too different from the sound her leg made when the alligator bit down.

～

She ran her hand along the back of her knee where the tooth

marks angled up and around like a crooked smile. Someone said her dad might go to jail for hitting the reporter.

Emily threw the remote across the room. The cover
broke off, and the batteries spilled out onto the floor.

"It happened like you said, right?" she asked, down
on her hands and knees scooping the batteries up.

"Yes ma'am."

"You didn't just cut your leg on an old car fender or
something?"

How weird was it that she missed the alligator. Like a
friend almost, someone who moved away one summer day
without telling her.

"No, I don't think so."

Emily blew the hair out of her face and grunted back
up onto the couch.

"Goddamn Florida is all I can say."

Out on Lake Mary Jane, a man with a long pole and
a pistol dragged an alligator out of the water. He said it
was the same one, but how would he know?

They sat together on the couch, her and Emily, with
an empty space between them. Anna could smell the but-
terfly bush outside the kitchen window that Emily always
left open and her dad yelled at her about. This was her fa-
vorite time of year, the flowers reminded her—everything
alive and stirring before summer came on full and it got
too hot to do anything at all.

They'd think she was crazy if she told them how
much she still loved swimming, the lake so cool and quiet.
She wanted to go back, maybe ask the gator why it had
let go. It wasn't her doing, she knew that. Like everyone
said, she was too little. All she knew was it had left its
mark on her, which is what love does.

CROSSING TO LOPEZ

THERE WASN'T AS MUCH SATISFACTION as I'd hoped in watching Jason fall. Seeing him suspended for a second after I'd tripped the latch—not falling yet, but knowing he was going to—I did enjoy that. But at the same time, I knew it wasn't progress. No matter what had happened over the years I should have moved beyond it. No matter that every rise of his was accompanied by a fall of mine, we were adults. I should have grown up, let the grievances fade between us. How else do you get past banging your head against a wall?

"Do you miss it?" my daughter asked just this morning, running her finger across my eye patch. When she was little, she would reach under the patch and touch the empty spot, gently. It never bothered her.

"Maybe sometimes."

A typical equivocation on my part that she fortunately has not inherited.

"I like it this way," she said.

It happened when we were in high school, me and Jason, crossing the Kendricks' pasture to try to catch their llamas copulating and take pot shots at them with a BB gun. Stuck out on an island in Juan de Fuca Strait, with nothing but water everywhere, that's what we had. He claimed it was an accident, that he was aiming at the tractor behind me. But we'd just split two Colt 45 talls and I was arguing with him about my girlfriend Tricia who would soon be his girlfriend, so yeah, I'm skeptical.

I didn't appreciate her sufficiently, he was saying, and he may have been right. (At school I'd come across them sometimes, leaning close, their eyes—two apiece—lingering on each other unapologetically.) As we crossed from the road through the greening fields with the malt liquor circulating freely among my suspicions, he extolled her virtues and my shortcomings, and I hated them both a little. I said she couldn't go a day without being told she was a precious gift, and if I still had the receipt I'd return her. And yes I did call her an emotional orca, but even I don't know what that means, so as justifiable cause it's pretty thin.

It didn't hurt, exactly. There was an ache and a weird feeling of subtraction, something yanked out of me, but that was it. A red-tail circling above the ridge screeched once, then faded out, dissolved into a gray amorphousness. Not black, like you might think, just a dull spreading opacity, which it remains to this day.

—

"I've always been fascinated by the decision-making

process," Jason said, standing in front of the classroom where his daughter and mine sat next to each other, watching rapt as he turned his mice loose in their glass box to ram into transparent doors and claw their way over Stickum-painted barricades. There was no cheese waiting for them at the end, which I had thought was customary and only fair. There was no prize at all, and no discernible way out. He set them going like balls rolling downhill, noting their choices, clicking his stopwatch to record their reaction times, knowing their journey would be without end or reward.

"We remove the reward so that each decision is a distinct event enacted for its own sake. A pure choice in isolation."

A few of the kids nodded, as if they knew what the hell he was talking about.

When it was my turn, I put some spreadsheets up on the projector, knowing full well that no kid would want to hear more about math on a day that was supposed to be a vacation from it. The numbers were meaningless artifacts from a time when I believed in balanced equations, butterflies pinned to a cork board. I closed with this:

"Infinity is the greatest achievement in mathematics history. Aside from zero."

We ate lunch with the kids at short metal tables bolted to the blacktop. My knee banged against the pipe brace every time I moved, and when the bell rang I limped off beside Jason and his mice into a light drizzle. My daughter gave me a hug. She didn't hold my presentation against me. How in the world do we deserve such generosity, I want to know.

~

Early on I considered a glass eye—Jason's idea, inciden-
tally—but that was a bust. There was a place in Seattle
that made them to order, custom colors, even patterns
and little overlaid pictures. Tricia might like to help pick
one out, Jason suggested—it would make her feel con-
nected to me, he said. I could get an eye that matched her
eyes, or went with her shoes, whatever. Not surprisingly, things didn't work out as he'd intimated. She saw the
socket for the first time and was repulsed. She slammed
her own eyes shut like security doors, pinched them tight
and turned away in disgust from my Sea of Intranquility.

—

The whistle sounded at the top of the grade, and we half-
jogged down to the dock. Jason looked natural doing it,
his arms swinging comfortably, his knees rising rhyth-
mically, while I shuffled awkwardly downhill. Owing to
my compromised depth perception, the road hovered in-
distinctly somewhere below me. My bones jarred against
one another as the ramp rose up and retreated again,
their connective tissue worn to threads. And then—for
the cyanide on the sundae—who should we meet on the
ferry?

Tricia gave Jason a big hug, studying me with a crin-
kled nose over his shoulder.

"What happened to you?"

"What do you mean?" I said.

She waved me off and separated from Jason, tugging
the ponytail poking out the back of her ball cap and making the odd little clicking sound she'd always made when
words failed her. The rain bounced off her spandexed
limbs as she cantered in place.

"I'm training for a triathlon." she said.

"Good for you," Jason said.

The water of the strait was almost black.

"Do you wear a wetsuit?" I asked.

"Some people do. I don't."

"Of course not."

She tried to glare at me, but her eyes kept flicking up to my patch, decorated today with a bright whirl of Fibonacci spirals. I moved closer to the rail. She and Jason whispered, their foreheads almost touching. They'd both been married to other people for some time, but if that meant the same thing to them that it did to most it would be a revelation.

I tried not to listen, focusing instead on the bow wave rolling out toward Canada in a white arc. We'd gone there once, the three of us. To Stanley Park. We'd tried to get lost, and nearly succeeded, stumbling onto the car at the end of the sea wall long past dark. Our island was a pale dot offshore, an afterthought. Tricia had been holding on more and more tightly to my hand as the day faded out and the temperature started to drop. Joined for good, I thought.

Just before we reached the car, Jason stumbled and wrenched his ankle. Tricia let go of my hand, and there he was between us—leaning his weight on me, his other arm looped around her neck.

"What kind of friend are you?" he said when I objected, prompting Tricia to give me the first of many looks of diminishing approval. On the ferry home, we went up to the lounge and drank coffee thick with sugar. Tricia rested Jason's foot in her lap. We seemed to be on two different boats after that, with mine listing badly and taking on water.

Now Jason was holding up his cage describing his success in the classroom, and they were both laughing. Tricia looked at me once, dismissively, from under her wispy bangs. Then she turned away and jogged off, her shoes squeaking on the wet deck, fading off toward the bow like scavenging gulls.

~

Against my will, I still see her sometimes naked beside me in our little cove on the west side of the island. She was beautiful, I have to admit, her skin like paper waiting to be written on, smooth and unmarked in the first good sun of the year. Her northern pallor translated as beauty against the gray rock, while mine came across as something sickly and deprived. She stretched languidly and rolled toward me.

"It's almost worth living here on days like this," she said. I agreed one hundred percent.

I was wearing a new patch, bright red with a gold-rimmed star in the center. She'd touched it playfully once or twice already—I didn't like it, but she was so open beside me it seemed ungracious to object. Then she started to lift it; I could feel it hinging like a secret door. I grabbed her wrist, squeezing harder than I meant to.

"I just want to see it again." she said.

"No you don't."

"It won't make any difference."

I don't know who she thought she was kidding.

She made the clicking sound, pulled her shirt closed over her perfect breasts and rolled away from me again. Something in the vicinity of my heart collapsed. The sun disappeared behind a cloud, and as far as I know never came out again.

She waited an appropriate period before dumping me, out of respect for her own sensitivity. She wasn't so shallow as to hold my infirmity against me—she insisted on that. It wasn't the sunken egg cup where my eye used to be she objected to, it was my inaccessibility. Though to most people's minds I'm as accessible as a *People* magazine. Meanwhile, somewhere not far away, Jason was waiting, all sympathy and hard-on. She complained, he commiserated. What a burden lifted I was! How had she stood it so long?

~

"How long do they live?" I asked.

"Who?" Jason said.

"The mice."

"I don't know. Four or five months, I guess."

"Is that normal?"

Jason nudged the box with his foot. "Do they suffer, you're asking."

I didn't know if that was what I was asking. Really I was just making conversation, but Jason never had much patience for digressions. Even crossing the Kendricks' pasture he took the straightest line. The trajectory of the BB to my eye was nothing if not direct.

"That's what kids usually ask," he said. "That's what they care about, and that's okay. I mean they're kids, I expect that. They're not going to care about reaction times, cortex development, autonomic versus somatic. I mean, come on."

"But I should."

"Well, look, it's survival. What separates us."

"Ah."

"You flinch or you don't flinch, and there you go."

"Yep. There you go."

I wondered if he'd ever tried to chase the neurons that go haywire when someone breaks your heart or stabs you in the back. If anybody had. That seemed like a sure bet for a grant.

Off to our side, a boat full of tourists sped along beside a small pod of orcas. The orcas looped and arced. Every time they turned, the boat turned. The people in the boat were bright orange in their life jackets, bunched on one side of the boat so that it listed unnervingly. We heard the captain bark something over the PA, and some of the orange blobs shifted back to the other side of the boat.

Jason smiled, leaning on the gate in the rail. He always stood there when he crossed, so he'd be the first one off at the other end. The gate rattled. The safety chain, normally clipped through a rusted hasp, dangled over the side and clanged against the hull.

"How's CeeCee doing?" he asked. "Better?"

"She's fine, yeah."

"Not everyone's cut out for . . . whatever. Success. Advancement."

He tapped the mouse cage with his toe and smiled again as the mice scrambled down their hallways, turned in desperate circles in their cul-de-sacs. After blowing into his cupped hands to thaw his fingers, he reached down and flipped open a trap door in the top of the cage.

"The kids seem to like her anyway," he said. "She's got Miss Congeniality sewed up, if nothing else."

With a little flourish like a magician—which is what I think he'd always seen himself as, conjuring traps and mazes from straight lines, making animate objects disappear with a wave of his hand—he snatched up a tiny, wriggling mouse and lifted it out. He held it by the tail, watching it arch its back and claw at the air with inadequate feet.

"The world divides up in essential ways," he said.

And with that he dropped the mouse over the side. A little white shape descending, bouncing once on the wake from the ferry and disappearing.

He smiled and made a mental note as if he'd learned something. His nose, pink in the cold, twitched. I wondered why we'd stayed on the same island all this time, bumping up against each other whichever way we turned. We could have left any day, either one of us.

It didn't take much. All I had to do was reach across and flip the latch; one finger, easy as that. Jason was leaning on the gate, hanging halfway over. His weight did most of the work. He went under only briefly before bobbing back up, eyes wide and bald spot showing. Tricia was there beside me again—as a vivid illustration of my backward progress—shaking me by the arm. I could see the spray of spit as she cursed me, red blotches on her cheeks, her chest heaving in fury as she reached up and yanked my patch off.

The triumph in her face as she brandished the patch like a scalp, shook it victoriously and threw it over the side, was something to see.

"There you are!" she screamed. "There you fucking are!"

True enough. True enough.

The tourists picked Jason up. He was a strong swimmer, even in wet clothes with a soaked jacket pulling him down, and something still stronger was pulling him in the opposite direction. It wasn't love for his wife or children, or the shadow of unheralded accomplishments, fame yanked away. No, he knew what I knew—this episode would cement my position on the island, deep in the shade of better men. It would be my last nail.

And what could I say? It was an experiment? I was studying him, timing him, noting the twitch of his lip, the fear in his eyes? Hardly.

He pointed a righteous finger at me, and everyone on the boat and on the ferry turned to look. I waved. A big, slow wave, like we were long lost friends who'd finally found each other again. Oh what the years had done to us! Oh the stories we could tell!

When we slowed on the approach to the dock, I reached down and clipped the chain back onto the gate. The rain was coming down harder, pinging off the deck and boiling the water down below. I tilted my head back and let it fall into the cup of my eye. It filled pointlessly, one drop at a time, like a battered artifact left behind by some long-dead civilization.

PARLIAMENT OF OWLS

A BRANCH BREAKING, A PUFF of breath. The owl pivoted toward the sounds, eyes widening, pupils dilating. The air had cooled quickly, the temperature dropping faster each day now once the sun had gone. There was a smell of impending snow, the mass of cold air pressing down. A grunt, something like a deer in panic. The owl's eyes black now, all pupil.

Tim Houck plunged deeper, knowing he was making a mistake. He'd been a Boy Scout before he was a minister, before he was a linebacker, before almost anything. He knew the thing to do was to wait. To talk yourself out of doing exactly what he was doing. He wasn't even sure now which way the car was. Make widening circles left until you cross your trail—that was the rule. Back then, of course, he hadn't been much interested in being found.

He could taste the gin when he breathed in, the dry

burn of it like paint fumes. He hadn't been drunk in some time. The crowd was all ex-jocks, so he knew going in what the reunion would be like. There was a certain stagnation common among them. They lived in the best of their gone moments, and pushed aside the worst. No one mentioned Ethan Coulter, for instance. And why would they? The only ghosts they believed in were their own better selves.

The air purred across the owl's soft flight feathers. Its ears, one higher on its head than the other, kept a pinpoint on the rustlings and surges. A shape materialized out of the dark, a large figure bent low and struggling. The owl veered off and lighted on the knob of a beech limb.

"For his years of service to excellence," Tim had said without laughing, as he'd preached salvation and dribbled half-hearted benedictions over lifeless parishioners without doing so. Hiding from his true duty in the same absent solemnity.

Coach Melton patted him on the ass as he stepped to the lectern—the standard football greeting. Tim watched him tear up, memorializing himself and the teams that had come and gone without a single championship. He was smaller than Tim remembered, less imposing. What he'd taken for authority must have been something else.

The owl preened and watched the man. The first flakes began to fall, as it had known they would, fat and heavy. The man stopped and looked up, made a series of noises.

"I repent for Ethan Coulter," he said, though he knew it wasn't worth much. When he could have done something, he didn't. The ribbing turning to punches.

A hard tackle called by coach, a concussion. Each step following the one before it in a way he couldn't get his feet to do now. It was strange, looking back, how it all fell into a narrative, the pattern plain as something sewn deliberately. At the time, it had been anything but that. A void of possibility.

He closed his eyes and concentrated, but it was impossible to call back the future that had been like an ocean washing against them. How had it shrunk to this?

Off to the owl's left, a rabbit stepped gingerly through a carpet of fallen needles. The owl swiveled its head to follow, then lost interest. The snow spun through the trees, driven this way and that by internal currents. Wet flakes settled on its bark-patterned back and melted on contact.

No. Someone had mentioned Ethan. Drew Brownfield; quietly, almost to himself. Coach's drink had frozen hallway to his cracked lips. Tim thought he might say something, but he only shook his head in mock mournfulness. There was a scholarship in Ethan's name now. Tim turned away and threw up on the gym floor.

"I was lost but . . ." he didn't finish the verse.

Deep in the owl's chest its breath gathered, its throat pouch puffed out. Hoo-ooo. The sound moved through the woods deflecting the falling flakes ever so slightly from their path, before becoming lost some distance off in the general stir of hidden things going about their business.

REPURPOSING

THE LIGHT DIDN'T HIT ALL at once. Resurfacing, mercifully, was a gradual thing. In the narrow hallway at the top of the shaft, thick skylights bathed him in a mellow green like the inside of an aquarium. Kyle always stayed there a few minutes before pulling his sunglasses on, taking a breath, and stepping out into the diffuse sun that tumbled down through hickory and pine and whatever else the woods were made of. He took another moment there to decompress, waiting for the thud of the lock engaging behind him. It always gave him a little sting of pleasure, the way it broke the silence. As the outside world gradually acclimated itself to him, he tucked his key card into his pocket and climbed on his bike. By the time the path emerged from the trees into full sun, he was ready for it—and, like a waking lizard, tilted his head back and soaked it in.

Carlynn and Lauren might have come from what she called the same narrow background, but Lauren still believed it was possible to rise above it. Calling their new regular The Albino, for instance—even if he really was awfully pale—the way Carlynn did, was just low class. Never mind that when he smiled, or tried to, his teeth showed yellow and the stubble on his cheeks gathered in patches sparse and uneven as a dying lawn. He was something her father would have scared her with when she was a child—a woods-thing, a night monster. Okay. Still he seemed, all in all, harmless enough.

She watched him lock his bike to the crepe myrtle in front of the shop. Nobody around Breedon rode bikes, except for the DUIs, so she didn't know who was going to steal it. He tugged on the chain twice, paused, then yanked it once more. Always the same. Maybe he was OCD. Everybody seemed to be now, any little superstition or habit was all of a sudden a disorder. Those poor ball players—if anyone looked too closely at them, they'd all be locked up. Rabbit's feet, years-old undershirts. Her brother had played all through high school, and held onto that way of thinking for a good while after: If I make this light, everybody will be okay for another year. If three grapes come off the bunch at once, I'll get that job. None of it worked, of course, but who did it hurt either?

When the little bell above the door chimed, she made a point of not looking up. She heard him move past, pausing for a second by the counter before making his way back to the graphic novels and strategy card games.

"Look at him," Carlynn whispered. "Sweating through his skinny-ass waistband."

REPURPOSING

Well, it was hot, hotter than most years—this early, anyway. Global warming, probably. Most people around Breedon didn't believe in it, of course, but that's just because they knew they'd have to change their habits if they did. Lauren believed. She believed in science, and she believed—always had—that people one way or another would end up ruining things. "We aren't as bright as we think," her father had said. "Just because you can teach somebody to drive a car or work a labeler, it doesn't mean they ought to be put in charge of anybody's destiny."

The heat poured through the windows and leaked under the door. She moved closer to the fan, let it blow through her hair and across her face, drying off the sweat stinging her eyes you could mistake for tears if you didn't know better.

～

Kyle flipped through *The Sandman*, tried to put himself into the story, right there in the panels the way he used to, but it wasn't working. He was afraid he was getting too old for it, for fantasy. Or maybe it was this place—out in the wilderness of western Kentucky. He still wasn't sure why he'd taken the job. He didn't care about computers anymore, there was no fascination for him in machines. The solitude was what had appealed to him, the idea of it. Finding some deeper part of himself through isolation and contemplation. A kind of digital Thoreau, that's how he'd framed his future self. It had felt good buying the three-pack of Moleskines—the bookstore clerk looked at him like someone consequential, a thinker. But he'd run out of thoughts in less than three pages, and the journals were now leveling the legs of his desk.

He picked up a bag of D&D dice, let them tumble

around in his palm. He could go for a game, but he had no friends here, didn't know anybody at all. When he thought about it, he hadn't made any new friends since sometime in junior high. And back then it had just happened. You fell together, like to like. In the adult world you had to make an effort, and he found it harder every year to work himself up to it.

"Seven fifty," the girl behind the counter said.

"Okay." He wanted to call her by name, say "Thank you Jane," or whatever. That was a step, wasn't it? He looked for a name tag, but realized he was just staring at her breasts—it would look like that anyway. He turned away, felt himself blush. The girl clicked her tongue like a teacher correcting him.

When he went to unlock his bike, he saw that somebody had stolen the saddle. He had to ride back to the data cave standing up, leaning out over the handlebars. He forgot at one point and nearly impaled himself— an emergency room story the staff would have laughed about for weeks. Who'd steal a goddamn bike saddle? Even here, in this backwater, the prevailing assholes unfailingly found him.

⌣

Carlynn came back from lunch laughing and carrying a bicycle seat.

"Boy's gonna get a surprise when he sits down," she said, waving the seat by its stem. Like it was a trophy of some kind, a slain creature.

"Why would you do that?" Lauren said.

"What? It's funny."

"That's some hospitality. Just think if you were him,

in some strange town—"

"Oh, it's strange."

"In some strange town, don't know anybody, and you get treated like that?"

Carlynn shrugged and dropped the seat on the counter. "You're no fun anymore."

Really, though, what kind of behavior was that, what brand of Southern hospitality did that fall under? And she was fun. That just wasn't her idea of it.

She lifted the seat off the counter and stowed it underneath with the case of plastic bags and the box of Swiffer pads. Its proximity embarrassed her a little. She thought about the way he'd blushed when he was checking her out. She didn't mind, really, it didn't happen all that often anymore. Everyone in town knew everybody else, they'd all grown up together, and there were no more surprises. People didn't even throw surprise birthday parties, they always fell flat. That, she thought, was the perfect town slogan for Breedon: Nothing Surprises Anybody.

He was a scientist of some kind, she'd heard, out at the Kipp Mine. What used to be the Kipp Mine. Which explained his pallor, the general inattention to appearance—he was working on something important, dedicating himself to a larger goal. In the interest of others, she was sure. Probably measuring the radiation penetrating into the old shafts, the rays chipping away at the earth like an ice pick. Working *on* something, not *for* something (or someone). To solve a problem, to better people's circumstances—not just to get a paycheck and a weekend.

And what was she doing? Selling gewgaws and comic books to redneck teens.

Carlynn offered to lock up, but the last time she did forty dollars disappeared from the till. Lauren had made the difference up herself, told Mr. Hantz it had gotten misplaced or fell behind the counter. Not again, though. As lousy a job as this was, she wasn't risking losing it to cover for somebody else's klepto tendencies. If Carlynn needed something, she could have come to her, or to Mr. Hantz. Now he suspected her, Lauren, straight as an arrow Lauren. He looked at her differently. That's what good deeds got you.

"I'll take care of it tonight," Lauren said. "You've got plans, right?"

"If I don't, I'll make some."

"Go on then."

Carlynn was slow getting her things together. She watched Lauren closely as she went about cashing out, running her tongue around inside her mouth like she did when she was thinking deeply. It was not attractive.

"Really," Lauren said. "Go have fun."

"Fun," Carlynn said, snorting. She seemed about to say something else, but instead she just turned and strolled out the door, her purse swinging at the end of her arm like she was on a boulevard somewhere—in Paris or something—and everybody was watching her. But it was just Breedon and only Lauren watching. She went back to counting.

~

She put the bike seat in her bag with the post poking out the top. She wasn't sure what she was going to do with it. The mine wasn't on her way home, but it wasn't completely out of the way either. Maybe she'd cut through the woods like she used to when she'd catch her dad after his shift, timing it so he'd be coming out of the elevator when she got there and she could straddle the bike and shuffle along beside him, kicking up dust nobody noticed, they were already so covered.

Gil Taver, who worked for the utility company, said the place sucked up power now like nobody's business. "Megawatts over everybody." Well, why not? Might as well make use of the place. The coal was long gone, and nobody wanted it anymore anyway. Solar was the thing now, and wind. Coal had never brought anybody anything but black lung and greenhouse gas. And towns like this, holes in the map.

The lights were on at the ball field. She could see little clots of teenagers out around the trees, their cars pulled up on the grass. Friday, the doubter's Sabbath. It didn't mean much to her now, but she still remembered. Drinking and necking under those same trees out along the first base line where she could see shadows moving and hear laughter and swearing. Nate's breath, whiskey-sharp along her skin. She hoped he was doing well now, she really did. But it wasn't likely. People didn't change, that was just a fantasy of little girls and drinkers.

Past where the road turned to gravel and the last of the lights were blocked by the trees, it was darker than she remembered. Of course, there were all those men with lamps on their helmets then—like explorers, bright eyes sweeping across the woods and the burned fringe of weeds. They seemed happy, that's the way she remembered it—a few singing even, high hillbilly voices—but that probably wasn't accurate. It was the end of coal already then, and no one had any illusions left.

81

"What's to stay for?" Nate had said that last night, leaning against his Camaro. Running a thumb along the little lip under the door handle. Caressing it.

"It'll come back."

"Coal? You're shitting me."

"Not coal, no. Breedon. Something else will come along."

"Like what?"

"I don't know. But places don't just die."

"Sure they do, all the time."

"They hibernate, maybe. Fall on hard times, but that's different."

"Where'd you get that?"

"It's history."

"Well, I'm talking about the future, not the past."

He didn't have anything better waiting for him when he drove off, she knew. A cousin somewhere in California, Bakersfield. She'd looked it up online, and it was even worse than Breedon. Dirt and dead grass, and oil pumps like rusted-out dinosaurs raising and dropping their heads, sucking the dry ground even drier.

She'd been right too, it had come back. Part way, at least. Businesses had stopped closing, a few new ones had opened up. There was an organic farm just outside of town now, a craft brewery with stainless steel vats shining in the window. And two coffee shops that sold drinks you'd never know were coffee. Of course, it could be that the rest of the country had just sunk a little lower, and they had only risen in relation. She couldn't be sure, but did it matter?

She turned the last bend and saw cars and people, headlights shining on the mine's scarred-up metal doors.

Big, bright rings like a Hollywood movie premiere or a prison escape.

~

Servers were going down right and left. He'd rebooted eight since lunch; the weekly average was four. He'd called the Data Center, and they'd yelled at him, told him to just fucking fix it. But this was way above his pay grade. He had no idea what to do, and he suspected they didn't either. He hadn't touched anything, it wasn't his fault—which didn't keep him from being a scapegoat. In fact, it was probably the perfect scenario for a scapegoat, maybe even the reason they'd hired him and sent him out here in the first place.

But that wasn't why he was crying. It was his bike, the stolen saddle. How stupid was that? Why should he care? Because it was personal, that's why. It wasn't a random crime, some fucked-up delinquent kid walking home from school. It wasn't a crime of opportunity, it was a hate crime. They hated him. He didn't know why, but they did. It had happened before, in other places, on other jobs. Something in him rubbed people the wrong way. If they got to know him, they'd like him—he knew they would—but he wouldn't get the chance. It had already passed. He was on the outside, and the door had slammed shut again in his face.

He punched the wall, solid rock that didn't give. He felt his knuckles crunch, the skin peel back. He was howling now like an animal trapped in its den.

Another row of LEDs went red, then another. Someone's data vaporized as he watched—family photos gone, a brilliant coming-of-age novel shredded into scrambled bits. Information all around him was spiraling out into blackness, like the arms of a galaxy gathering nothingness up in its sweep. Chaos, electronic Alzheimer's, loss and decay.

Then a knock, the void's fist rapping.

He wiped his nose and slunk over to the security console. The camera was the cheapest you could get, and she was pretty blurry, but it was definitely her. The girl from the store.

He pressed the intercom.

"Hello," he said.

She looked around comically.

He pressed the intercom again: "The button by the door."

"Sorry."

"That's okay."

"Look, there's some people out here. They're kind of unruly."

He could see a small crowd behind her haloed by headlights, the silhouettes of beer bottles and mullets and—was that a rifle?

"Why?"

She was yelling something at the crowd, then she turned back, half-smiled up at the camera.

"Sorry. What?"

"Why are they unruly?"

"It's Friday."

"I don't have any money or anything."

"They think you're the government, some secret part of it. Or there's aliens in there. Or something. I'm not too clear on it myself."

A bottle hit the wall beside the camera, spraying liq-

uid across the lens. The girl held her hand up to her forehead, brought it away and looked at it.

"Are you bleeding?" he said.

He could see her mouth moving, but there was only
white noise and a high piercing whine.

~

He felt the slowness of the ancient elevator's ascent as a
physical pain: "Come on come on come on," thumping the
heel of his hand against the panel. Rising up through the
darkness to—what? A mob of shadows shuffling through
a fog of dust and truck headlights.

"EVERYBODY CHILL THE FUCK OUT!" he
yelled, emerging into the relative glare.

A shadow or two paused to look at him, somebody
laughed and was shushed.

"Okay," a guy said—twenty-something in a Skrillex
t-shirt and cargo pants. "Will do."

Off to the side, the girl from the store sat on a blanket with a sterile pad pressed against her head.

"Are there aliens in there?" somebody in the back
asked.

"What?"

"In the mine."

"No, it's computers. Servers."

"Oh shit, really?" Skrillex said.

"Yes."

"Okay, makes sense. Nice and cool in there, wide
open."

"Right."

Skrillex leaned down, looked at the girl closely.

"You feeling all right? No concussion symptoms or

anything?"

She shook her head.

"Really sorry about that, Lauren. It was Cliff, he's an idiot. But you know that."

"Everybody knows that," somebody said. "Even Cliff."

"Fuckin' A," somebody else—presumably Cliff—said.

He could feel his knees shaking. If he talked now, his voice would come out thin and warbly, scared sounding. So he just nodded and squatted down beside the girl on the blanket. People were already moving off, cars backing out. Soon it was just the three of them.

"Underground, and they call it the cloud," Skrillex said finally.

"I know."

"Around here, man, it figures."

He produced a bottle of Jack Daniels from somewhere and set it on the blanket.

"Look, y'all take this, okay? And no hard feelings. Really, we've got nothing against the cloud."

"Or you either," somebody else said, a girl back in the shadows he couldn't see.

"Right, or you either."

Lauren—that was her name, he knew that much now—sat up on the blanket and squinted into the darkness.

"Was this your idea, Carlynn?"

No answer, just the sound of feet shuffling across gravel.

"You should be ashamed!"

Skrillex nodded in commiseration, then strolled back

to his car. They could hear the girl giggle as he climbed in beside her and they drove off.

Lauren reached into her purse and pulled something out. She was so close he could almost touch her.

"I brought your seat," she said. He didn't correct her, tell her it was actually a saddle. Not too long ago he would have.

~

He took her with him down a branch tunnel while he rebooted six more servers that had crashed, waiting for the sky to fall, for red lights to flare up and down the mine. Staring him down before pouncing. But that was it, the end of the emergency. Everything went green after that and stayed green. He had no idea what the glitch had been—an act of god, sun spots, voodoo.

"You live down here?" she asked. His cot and his little bookshelf were wedged against the wall under an old vent pipe. It looked like a dungeon, he could see that.

"Pretty much. If you call it living."

"What do you call it?"

They spread the blanket out on the floor. He could feel the heat of the processors washing over them, the whiskey firing through his brain. There were pockets of safety in the world, he was beginning to believe, cozy little corners amid the melee.

~

She'd be fired first thing Monday. She knew it as surely as if it had already happened. Mr. Hantz would see the pictures, maybe on Carlynn's phone—Lauren with her head bleeding, yelling and waving a bottle. He'd hear about the scuffle from his police friends. By tomorrow it would be a riot, and he wouldn't want any part of it. Lauren couldn't imagine who else he'd get to work in the crummy little store, but that was his problem. She was safe in the mine for now. Safe and sound in a hole in the ground, as her father used to say.

The boy was looking at her in a way she recognized. He took a big slug of the whiskey, choked a little on it. He was so awkward that a twinge of something like mercy shivered through her. He leaned in, knocking the whiskey over.

"Sorry," he said.

"Hold on," she said, righting the bottle.

"I'm sorry. I'm not too good at this."

She took another sip, scrunched up her face.

"Nobody is."

No one she'd ever known, at least. Maybe her mother and her father had the knack once, that mutual feeling, but that was a long time ago—and as far as she knew she'd spoiled it. It was just her and her dad for most of her life, then he'd died in the mine . . . could anyone blame her for having her doubts?

"I was with this one guy for a while," she said. "We almost got married."

Nate another in the line of disasters, but without all the dust and frenzy; just a steady drift apart that always made her think of icebergs—clumsy and slow and inevitable.

"We were okay at this part of it," she said. "But it's more than that, isn't it? A relationship."

"I don't know."

"No," she agreed. "Me neither."

She lay back on the rock floor. The cave ceiling arched out of sight overhead; above that was everything and everyone else. She let them all go. After a little while he moved closer, rolled half onto her and started kissing the side of her head. His chin poked into her neck. The floor was uneven, and he was heavy on top of her, not as light as he looked. All sharp points, hip bones and knees.

Along the walls little green lights glowed, cycling on and off like animals' eyes. She squinted, let them dissolve into vague, amorphous blobs and thought: What if it *was* just us left? All alone down here, everything up above blown up or melted or dried out. No Carlynn, no Nate, no Mr. Hantz. Just me and—she didn't even know his name. The Albino, but she couldn't very well call him that. She'd have to ask him later. He was busy now, breathing hard.

When you thought about it, it had already happened—on a small scale, and more than once. Little armageddons when people moved away or died, your world skewed off a little. Towns went under, like this one, and if they came back it was never the same.

She closed her eyes, felt herself spinning. She hoped this wasn't really the end, or some new beginning. Fumbling around in a cave with the ghosts of all the people lost in whatever disaster floating through the air above them. She saw her father marching hand-in-hand with the other dead miners in a long line down toward the chiseled-out face, past rows of machines humming and whirring, right through the rock, jagged and ancient, waiting patiently for its next incarnation.

She kicked her foot against a plastic bin: "REDUCE, REUSE." She giggled, and he stopped for a second. She stifled herself, and he started up again. She whispered a name, even though it was just a guess and couldn't possibly have been his: "Henry."

Some familiarity was called for, after all. Some attempt, however clumsy, at picking up the thread. He looked at her.

"I'm Kyle."

"Kyle?"

"Yeah."

"Okay."

She pulled his head down onto her shoulder.

"Who's Henry?" he said.

"Nobody."

His breath was warm against her collarbone, coming in ragged bursts, all the tension and thrill gone suddenly out of him. He might have been crying, she wasn't sure; she hugged him as best she could. How was she supposed to tell him about the guy she'd seen in her mind a thousand times, walking toward her with a hand raised and a big smile, opening his mouth to ask her where she'd been all his life.

THE MIDDLE GROUND

HE CLAIMED HE WAS AIMING where he hit me, but I don't buy it. I was moving through trees, cutting downhill—he wasn't that good. Granted, he did find me, tracked me through some pretty unforgiving country. I watched him doing it, saw the careful way he stepped alongside my trail, the almost delicate way he slung his rifle. The smile too, when I went down. All of it familiar in a way I'm sure he didn't understand. It was the little things that reminded me of his mother, and I told him so.

"She squinted like that when she got excited."

"Leave her out of this."

I tried to explain our history to him, the nights riding in my car up to the bluffs above the river where we could look out and beyond our puny little home. The itch we both had that she was the first to scratch.

"She was beautiful," I said, and not just to soften him

91

up, to get him thinking about letting me go. It was true. I wanted him to understand what it was like for us to be young who weren't any more. The way we just went where we felt like—up into the mountains, out to the coast—no plans or maps. I wanted him to see us how we were when it was a new day every day, with the sun bright and blinding, how we saw each other before our eyes adjusted to the light.

"She never mentioned you," he said.

It was a disappointment, I'll admit, to think I'd never come up. I had imagined at some point she'd have wanted to pass her full self on. If you don't show your kids all of you, how are they going to do better?

"Doesn't mean she wasn't thinking about me."

He considered that.

"It doesn't mean she was either."

He was one of those, who can't see any farther than the negation of something. No nuance, no middle ground.

"She never disappeared on you? In the car maybe when a certain song came on, or looking out a window at the leaves changing?"

"It's all pines where we are."

"She must miss it."

He laughed and shook his head.

"You think nobody's tried this before? Humanizing is what we call it."

"That's what everybody calls it."

"It doesn't work."

He'd taken a job that made him narrow his field of view, with no idea what he'd traded off. I felt sorry for him. Still, it seemed he gave a little more care to binding my shoulder than he might have otherwise.

⌒

He'd chased me quite a distance, almost to Canada. I'd recognized him right off, even bundled up and Kevlared. But don't think I let him catch me—he wasn't a little kid that had to be let win, and I'm not so sentimental I'd surrender to prison just so we could have our heart-to-heart. I'd gotten old and slow, is all, and had maybe lost some of the motivation he still had.

The nearest road was a good ten miles away, so I told him about some of our trips, his mother's and mine, as we walked out—skiing off into the untracked nothing, the emptiness like a cold drink; her lying naked on a rock sunning herself, a vision in an unbroken expanse where nothing moved but my eyes taking her in. Thinking of the recounting as a favor to her. I didn't tell him about the way she tore me down little by little, how she would visit me after we'd broken up and hardly say a word. Come to me at her lowest, where she could be the northern star and not just another guttering match.

A gust out of the north scooped handfuls of loose snow off the trail and into our faces.

"She still hate the wind?"

He turned and looked me up and down again.

"When it blows up like this," I said, "and the trees all start rattling, I think about how it used to scare her. I never found out why, I never understood it."

"You don't have anything to do with her."

"I do, though. I wish you were right sometimes, believe me."

Another gust slammed us, knocking him sideways. I could have made a move, he knew that, but I didn't. He saw it and relaxed a little.

"It still scares her," he said.

I nodded, reassured there was still a part of the past close enough you could just about touch it. A half-smile I half recognized flashed across his face.

"It'd be hard to find a windier place than she picked," he said.

"That's true, isn't it? Why do you think she'd do that?"

"To look it in the eye, I guess."

And right there, that was it. He'd nailed it. It made me feel a little easier toward her—and him—picturing her standing outside her house, watching the wind come across the Palouse carrying dust and torn wheat heads and who knows what all. Listening to it build and build, wanting to run but fighting it with everything she had. Holding her ground to show her only son there wasn't any door you could close tight enough as the one leading into your heart.

DICK FLEMING IS LOST

GEORGE WASN'T FRIENDS, EXACTLY, WITH Dick Fleming. He knew him well enough to nod to in the halls and, later, at the meeting house. He thought Kip might remember him, might even have kept in touch, but all he said was "sort of a washout, wasn't he?" Which bothered George more than he would have imagined. It wasn't a fitting way for anyone to be remembered.

He opened the alumni bulletin again, hoping it was more helpful this time—that more detail had been added while he wasn't looking, as happened from time to time. It was a phenomenon he didn't understand, or question overmuch. How he could see a thing in one way—the view out a window, an illustration in a book—then later, going back, find it changed in some small respect. Elizabeth put it down to absent-mindedness, but George had come to believe—though he'd never say it—that things were less fixed than people understood.

This time, nothing had changed. Dick Fleming was still lost.

Class of 1926

Dick Fleming is lost. When last heard from he was living at Hotel Olhm, Martinez, California. Any information about his whereabouts will be appreciated.

Hotel Olhm? What kind of a name was that, Olhm? It seemed a made-up one, something arrived at by shaking letters in a dice cup.

George took an atlas down from the bookshelf, opened it to California. The map took up two pages. He had assumed, by the sound of it, that he'd find Martinez in the south, down in the brown and wrinkled desert section of the map. Somewhere close to Mexico. But it was much farther north, near San Francisco. Where, by contrast, fat blue lines abounded, merging into amoebic blue masses spreading like a living thing, parting and joining such that it was hard to tell whether the land enclosed the water or the water was in the process of consuming the land. George would have put his money on the water.

Elizabeth had been enamored of California when they were first married, before the bank runs and soup lines. She'd lobbied him to take her there, describing their imagined journey vividly: The sway of the train like a ship, the land passing in endless variety—prairies and lakes and mountains—while they sat in the dining car and watched. Appreciative and aloof, it had seemed to him, hardly a part of it at all.

"What would we do there?" he'd wanted to know. Which had struck her as an insulting question. Getting there was the point. Having an adventure. "We'd just turn around?"

He didn't recall her response. A sigh, he imagined, and an angry exit. But now, he understood—or thought he did. When she got home from her bridge group that night, he was waiting up.

"I'm ready now," he said.

"For what?"

"California."

She'd just laughed, as he must have known she would. The idea of California was as much a part of their past as any of the other things they'd discussed and discarded when they were young enough to act and failed to.

The train lurched out of the station, shaking a bag loose from someone's arms. A small bottle of dark liquor was snatched up quickly, having somehow remained intact in the fall. A miracle, the man who'd dropped it must have thought. Such was the state of miracles at present. George turned back to the window to watch the trees give way to open farmland and, in the distance, a clutch of puffing stacks. The smoke from the stacks hung low over the intervening fields, throwing a wide, ragged shadow across them. The ride in this direction was always the same, light into dark.

How had Dick Fleming made his decision—if it had been a decision, and not just circumstance carrying him along. Perhaps it had been a job that didn't pan out, a company that had gone under like so many others. A lost opportunity before he'd even stepped off the train. George pictured him knocking on a wide, heavy door, waiting in vain for a man in a suit to answer, a fat man swollen with optimism and rosy forecasts. Then sitting on the curb, thinking: maybe everyone's gone to lunch. The sun dropping slowly behind him, reflecting off the water until the water turned black and he picked up his suitcase and began looking for somewhere to stay.

Decisions came harder to George. How many days and nights of waffling, back and forth, would he have gone through before boarding that train to Martinez? There was so much uncertainty in any proposition, finding a single right answer was next to impossible. It drove Elizabeth mad, almost to tears at times. But who could say now he'd been wrong to weigh his arguments so carefully, to favor the safer choice, when Dick Fleming—who maybe hadn't—was lost.

Mr. Pitcall was out, as George had known he would be, when he made his way to the Train Manager's office. Another emergency meeting. Claire helped him locate the number to the Hotel Olhm, and put in the call.

The connection was poor, with a steady whine like mosquitoes swarming at his ear. The voice on the other end was faint and watery. He saw the atlas again, the pervasive ingress of blue.

"I'd like Dick Fleming's room, please."

"Let me check."

More water and mosquitoes, the far end of the line a swamp lapping around the Hotel Olhm.

"I don't see him."

"No, of course. But . . . sorry, is he registered there?"

"I don't see him," the desk clerk repeated.

George raised an eyebrow at Claire, shook his head faintly.

"May I ask if he has been registered," George said. "Recently."

"People come and go," the man said.

"I understand."

"It's the nature of the business, really. No fixity."

George weighed his response to that, but before he could formulate one the man was gone. Hung up, or the line failed. The Hotel Olhm, perhaps, finally succumbing to the flood.

"No luck?" Claire asked.

"No fixity."

"Fixity?"

"That's what he said."

"Huh. I guess that's that, then."

"I guess it is," George said, knowing full well that was not that. He hadn't expected to find Dick Fleming so easily. He was lost, after all. It was doubtful the bulletin editor—Chub Neely, Class of 1928—would have said so if he hadn't expended some minimal effort at locating him. And by the way, why lost? Wasn't it explorers who were lost, or shipwrecks? Not classmates, even unremarkable ones, just setting out. Amid an established populace.

That afternoon—when he should have been reworking the road maintenance schedule to account for the men let go during the week—he wrote a letter to Chub Neely. Asking, among other things, how he had arrived at the conclusion that Dick Fleming was indeed "lost." Where did he get the name of the Hotel Olhm? Had someone crossed paths with him in Martinez?

Chub would, of course, wonder what his interest was

and ask questions in return. Bulletin housekeeping questions, but nonetheless prying: How long had George been married? Did he have any children? Who were his wife's family? Was it a crushing disappointment to be passed over, to have your father hand his company's reins to someone else? George crumpled the letter up and threw it away. Then retrieved it, tore it up, and threw it away again.

He worked on the schedule, knowing the job was impossible, that the tide was against them. How could the backlog of repairs and upkeep possibly get done if they continued laying off crews? Eventually there'd be an accident, and someone would take the blame. It wouldn't be Pitcall.

His mind persisted in wandering through the day, and each time it did there was Dick Fleming. George saw him with a clarity of imagination that was foreign to him. Flights of fancy were not his strength. Never once, that he could remember, had he set himself down in as thoroughly imagined a place as the steep, hide-brown hills Dick Fleming was now ascending in switchbacks. In full summer, evidently, the sun dazzling and merciless directly overhead. The back of Fleming's shirt was dark with sweat, the suitcase in his hand fraying at its seams, the halves held closed with a cross of twine.

He stopped at a flat spot by a rock outcrop and looked back the way he'd come. Sweat ran into his eyes and he blinked it away. Far below, he could hear a door slamming in the wind off the strait. The door of some vast, empty warehouse, maybe Fuchs & Co. Its mouth gaping as it had when he'd walked around the corner that second morning to find it weeks out of business, rust already working its way across the rows of empty shelves.

When the job had first been broached, he'd moved down to Delaware for a time to be near the water. Twice a day he'd ridden the Cape May ferry over and back to get the feel of a ship under him, so that when he boarded the international freighters coming into port to perform his inspections he wouldn't be laughed off. He'd have his sea legs under him. He had imagined Martinez, exotic and new, free of all the history that crowded into every corner of the East. Lost battles and won wars cloaked in verdigris, stiff old customs rubbing his will raw.

Something rustled off to his left. He turned to see a coyote coming over the crest of the hill—he presumed it was a coyote, what else could it be? It stopped and sniffed the air. Its belly looked caved-in, its ribs like a corset cinched tight and hurriedly draped in dun hide. When it spotted him, it lurched to one side as if kicked. It backed away over the brow of the hill, never taking its eyes off him. Dark, sunken eyes that anticipated nothing but misfortune. Dick Fleming picked up his bag and started up the hill again.

A whistle sounded in the yard. George looked up at the clock. He'd missed his train.

~

Elizabeth would expect him, but wouldn't be worried; he was sure of that. Even when the dinner went cold and she had the girl from next door take it away. Elizabeth had hired her to cook for them, dinners only, without asking him. He'd hoped she would understand, without George having to point it out, that they couldn't really afford the girl. Maybe she could try her hand at it again, she'd only get better. To which Elizabeth would have replied that she had no wish to get better, that being good at something like cooking was almost a disgrace.

He slowed as he passed The Cobbles, stole a glance through the window. He was quite hungry, his lunch had been a single spindly leg of overcooked chicken. Looking up from a plate of roast beef and scrod, he found Mr. Pitcall watching him from the bar. Mr. Pitcall! He was three years younger than George. By all rights he should have been Tommy, and George should have been Mr. Evans. George nodded, hoping that would be enough. But Pitcall waved him inside, mouthing "Get in here."

"You're a lucky man, George."

"Very much," George said.

"You might have had my job. Might have spent your evenings here." He swept his arm around the room, knocking over the empty glass beside his half-full one.

"I never much cared for it. All this. I like a clear head and a quiet room."

"I'm not surprised."

"We each have our preferred ways. That's all I'm saying."

"Preferred ways of what?" Pitcall asked. "Kicking time along? Running out the clock?"

It was unseemly, his complaining like this. George's father would have thought twice if he could see him now.

"Your implication, I take it," George said, to his own surprise, "is that it's all been for the best. I should be grateful."

"Is that what I'm saying?"

"You got the short end, despite appearances."

Pitcall squinted at him.

"Are you getting a backbone?"

"It's distasteful, is all. Sitting here like this, with all this. People are lost, genuinely lost out there."

"And now you're a priest to boot."

George pounded his fist on the bar, sloshing the bourbon from Pitcall's glass. Pitcall watched the dark spill spread on the wood.

"People count on you," George said.

Pitcall grabbed his sleeve as he rose to leave. George looked at his hand, the white knuckles and prominent veins. Almost an old man's hands. Pitcall let go.

"If you see your father's ghost," he said. "Tell him thank you from me."

"He thought you deserved it."

Pitcall laughed, a harsh laugh that degenerated into a hacking cough.

"Maybe I do," he said, when the fit had nearly passed.

George tried to judge his location by small signs as the train rattled through the dark—the double thump of a switch being crossed, a glimpse of starlit field. His reflection in the window was a distraction; the eyes, above all, that went where he went. He lowered the window, ignoring the complaints from behind him as wind whistled into the car. Outside, everything was settling into stillness. Only a faint ripple rolled out as they passed, lifting the trackside growth like a sheet of paper being torn off.

～

During the night, a thunderstorm passed close by. It didn't wake him or Elizabeth, but it found its way into his sleep. He could feel the shape of it, somehow familiar—a hand, he thought at first, but no; less distinct. It moved across the length of his body, cool and gentle, rustling the leaves outside his window, laying the thinnest veneer of stars across the night sky. The next morning, the smoke had lowered even further, obscuring everything taller than a house. The sun was a dim, amorphous glow behind it, but George felt awash in light. He would act, he'd decided, for once. He would telegraph the police in Martinez and report Dick Fleming missing.

"Did you know him?" Elizabeth asked over breakfast.

"Not well."

"So then . . . ?"

"People need help sometimes."

"Of course. But even so, would he ask you, of all people?"

"What's wrong with me?"

Elizabeth puffed out an impatient breath.

"You have enough to worry about."

George would have liked to hear her inventory; he didn't think their lists would tally.

He'd found a picture of Dick Fleming in the Epitome, their yearbook. Some years would naturally have been added, his hair maybe flecked already with gray. Doubt might have found its way into his grin, but he would still be, for police purposes, identifiable. George looked at the picture again—was there something there, in that captured moment, that might have anticipated this present one? The smoke moved past his window like the underside of some foul sea; he could sense him out there, lost and wandering, waiting for someone to call out. Like a boy playing blind man's bluff after everyone had gone home. All except George. George was still here, and he would call his name and lead him back.

DICK FLEMING IS LOST

A sudden scream of brakes threw him forward. He braced his arm against the seatback, the train shuddered to a stop. The porter did his best to calm everyone, but had little useful information to impart. Despite the ripple of panic passing through the car, for the first morning in some time George rose with confidence from his seat. The porter nodded to him, touched the brim of his cap. George smiled and nodded back. They were all on the same team, weren't they? Though it was true that only one of them spent all day on his feet, and at the end of the day they went home to quite different neighborhoods.

They were just shy of Wye Station, Pitcall's stop. George patted the porter on the shoulder as he passed, and stepped down onto the road bed. He could see the brakeman and engineer beside the engine up ahead. There was a smell of burned metal drifting back, and something else. George felt a current of dread push against him. He knew—he was unaccountably sure of it—that Tommy Pitcall was at the head of the train, dead on the tracks.

The porter was at his side, touching his sleeve.

"You'd better come to the front, Mr. Evans."

George nodded, but didn't follow the man stepping carefully along the tie ends toward what was surely a violent and bloody scene. "It's out of our hands," he wanted to say, but instead simply turned the other way. It had never been in their hands, was the simple truth. Very little had.

He walked along the tracks a short distance, past the rear of the train, then turned into the woods. He tried to compose a kind of eulogy for Tommy, but could only think how like him it was to make his death a burden to so many. He remembered something about Dick Fleming then—a funeral passing down the street beside the school, the kids all come out to watch. The road was still dirt back then, and the funeral wagon was drawn by two big draft horses. One of the horses spooked at something, pulling the wagon roughly sideways. Dick Fleming brushed past him, shouldering him hard, and took the horse by its bridle. He held its head while it lifted him off the ground and slammed him back down, talking to it, until it settled enough for the driver to regain control. George only heard one thing he said during the ruckus—"calm your heart, calm your heart"—an odd phrase, but nothing more than that.

Afterward, everyone cheered him and slapped him on the back, but he didn't seem to care. George found out later it was Dick's own mother in the coffin, and was ashamed of the jealousy he'd felt in the face of Dick Fleming's heroics.

There was an old trail that followed along the edge of the pond, over Willow Creek and up through the pines at the bottom of their land. His shoes were soaked through and his jacket flecked with needles and dead leaves when he emerged from the treeline. He stopped at the fringe of their lawn to brush himself off, make himself presentable. Elizabeth would wonder what he was doing home at this hour. He would tell her that life was short, that he wanted to take her somewhere beautiful and foreign. Not forever, but for a while. There was still so much of each other they had to discover.

The drapes were half open, and he could see her moving back and forth beyond the window. She hadn't seen him yet. Her movements were strange, not quite natural. It took him a moment to realize she was dancing. Her head swayed, her hips moved slowly side to side. Her hair was down, which somehow accentuated her nakedness. He watched her in wonder, enchanted, until Tommy Pitcall entered the frame beside her. He put his hands on her waist. They glided through the room—her breasts lifting and falling, his prick flouncing—as if no one else mattered. Which, he supposed, they didn't.

Off to the east, as he stepped back into the woods, he could hear the train starting up again. He didn't give much thought now to what had caused it to stop. It hadn't been Tommy Pitcall.

"Another hobo," Pitcall would say to Claire the next day.

"A person, then."

A cursory investigation would be done, but it would be impossible to determine whether the man had stepped purposefully onto the tracks or had simply not heard the train coming. It happened both ways.

George walked west, away from the rail line. It would be easy enough to avoid the villages and townships, they were still small and separated widely out that way. The camps, the makeshift towns in between, would surely take him in.

As his home grew smaller and less plausible behind him, George thought of San Francisco—a place he'd never been, though Dick Fleming likely had. Specifically, he considered the turntables. Claire had visited the city as a young girl, and it was from her he'd heard about them; how the famous cable cars were turned by the passengers themselves—a mass of people with no connection to one another pushing together until the car revolved a full one hundred and eighty degrees. It was remarkable, really.

Here they simply shuttled the engine to the other end of the train. It was easier by several factors, certainly more practical. But there was more than that at stake, surely.

At some point he realized he was still carrying the yearbook. He cleared a hollow beside a dry stream bed, dropped the book in and covered it over. Dick Fleming had escaped its pages. If he was found tomorrow, it would be as a different man—an engineer, an artist, a father, husband, friend—a man with a ready laugh and a firm handshake, late of the Hotel Olhm. And who, George wanted to know, was he to deny anyone that?

THE NEW CANAAN VILLAGE FOR EPILEPTICS

PEOPLE FIND IT DIFFICULT TO believe there ever was such a place, even though it's more or less still here. The name's changed, of course. That seems to be what people objected to most. It perpetuated our stigma, they said. But it was a home, regardless of the name, a place where we could go about our business ungawked at. There were walkways and gardens, a bandstand above the creek. There were lives being lived, both well and poorly. It was a world, in other words, nearly like any other.

Our illness was scarcely considered at the time, much less understood. There were no medications then to control the seizures. The sight of one of us writhing and spitting was unsettling for the general population, so we were sequestered. Before the village, we were exiled to mental institutions, to languish with the schizophrenics and depressives with whom we shared a mutual defect:

we were inconvenient. To our discredit, we looked down on them just as the world outside looked down on us.

If we were lucky, the seizures would come in private, away from judging eyes. Many would go months, sometimes years, between episodes—all we could do was wait, to try to hear the whirring of our nerves, to anticipate the coming chaos.

⌒

When Felicia arrived at the village, I'd been a resident nearly a dozen years. It was I who organized the crew to overlay the original hard surfaces with wood chips, I who muted the lights and built the celebrated promenade along the creek, the Grand Mall. It was there, in fact, that I first met Felicia. A warm evening in May, fireflies lighting the creekside grass. A parade of waterfowl migrating overhead. She was beautiful in the way that a leap of faith is beautiful, those decisions that pronounce us most emphatically ourselves.

She kept a precise distance between us at all times as we walked. Stepping carefully, I noticed, almost levitating beside me. It was midway across the Japanese bridge, at the height of its sweeping arc, that she stopped suddenly and let out a cry—a high peal, like an animal with one foot caught in a trap. The seizure followed almost immediately.

She fell slowly to the ground, grasping at whatever was closest to hand—in this case, and often afterward, some part of me. Her seizures, it always seemed, were the embodiment of a deeper struggle: In her tautened face one could see her determination to remain Felicia, to hold herself separate from the spasms that shook her body.

Her eyes were a swirl of blue and gray, with brown flecks like a brook trout's distributed throughout. In them I beheld planets colliding, stars exploding to nebulae. The universe contained within, struggling to be born.

When it was over, she brushed herself off and rose gracefully to her feet, and we continued on. The next night we repeated our promenade (seizure included), and the night after that. And again, one night into another, until all the nights of our courtship coalesced into one long night lit by the waxing and waning moon and the yellow glow of the sodium lights.

~

James was born on the winter solstice, and Felicia went the entire delivery without a seizure. The day after as well. Up until then they had been daily occurrences, as regular as our prepared meals. The change alarmed her. She remained in a heightened state of vigilance throughout that first month of nursing and broken sleep—it was, in a sense, both an astonishing gift and a perplexing loss she had to acclimate herself to.

As the seizures remained at bay, and James grew, the cosmology of our love changed. It was something within me, she came to believe, that had caused her wiring to scramble. Never mind all that had come before, the episodes that preceded my appearance—the mind latches onto hope like a baby to a nipple.

In time she began to doubt her onetime vulnerability, the condition we had shared fading gradually into abstraction. One afternoon I looked up from my writhing to see her pressed into a corner of the kitchen, clutching James tightly to her breast. So it was that, when the medications began appearing, I volunteered for every trial. Suffered through nausea, vertigo, dissociation, only to be told that my particular variant was not amenable to treatment.

I watched my wife and child closely, as did Doctor Pence, the staff neurologist. After three years James was deemed unaffected, and Felicia cured. Doctor Pence was elated at the outcome. As was I, though my joy was tempered by inevitable sadness. In my experience, one rarely comes without the other. Felicia and James left on a Saturday, bright sun through the sycamore leaves, the grass unnaturally green. They each gave a quick wave before turning to face determinedly away from the village.

~

Enough suffering is thrust upon us that it's foolish to compound it with pain of our own making. Still, it's all but impossible to simply carry on when I see them everywhere: crossing the Japanese bridge, in the broken shade of the meadow, in the soft footing of the wildly overgrown trails. I should be grateful, I know, that they are together, out in the wider world. Going about their tremorless lives in some quiet town far away from our quaking village. Free, as it is sometimes—and perhaps correctly—called.

For me, the village is home as nowhere else has been, though it has grown derelict over the years since. There's rot in the bridge railing, weeds rampaging through the once verdant herb beds. Its decay is perhaps a reflection of those few of us left, and of the times that delivered us here. There are cures, as Doctor Pence says, and then there are cures.

SOGNSVANN

SUMMER WAS GOOD AND GONE now, and that was fine with Mad. What a relief it was with winter coming, sweaters and coats and hats. She flipped her collar up; she could smell snow. By tonight, certainly.

Her father was in his chair, his bad leg up on the ottoman, dozing in front of the TV. There was the whiff of frying oil, a little fish, a trace of smoke from the cigarette he thought he'd gotten away with.

It wasn't a bad place to come home to, really. The books and the carvings, the window looking out on the hillside. The big oak door he'd lugged back from a little town way up north, that closed so solidly and tightly that not a breath from outside could make its way in.

He stirred, squinted up at her.

"Did you remember the cake?"

She shook her head.

"That's all right. No one really needs cake."

The big yellow chair sagged slightly beneath her, the fabric of the arms rough under her fingers from years of her mother's fidgeting. Other than little things like that, and a few pictures scattered around, she was gone so completely it was breathtaking.

"I could go back out," Mad said.

"You could," her father said. "But if you step in the same tracks too often, sooner or later you'll get stuck."

She considered going anyway. It was their anniversary, after all, her mother and father's. Forty-six years, it would have been.

It wasn't far to Konditori Pascal, perched on the brow of its hill like a gull. She'd even picked a tall almond cake out in the window when she'd passed earlier, the café crowded with students slashing the air with emphatic gestures and laughing over things dead Greeks and Romans and Englishmen had said. Their assurance through the glass was almost blinding, like a religious painting. She'd wanted to go in, she really had, but she'd caught her reflection in the window and it was obvious to anyone that she was something else entirely, small and mousy, almost lost in the slanting light. It was impossible for so many reasons, so she'd turned away and kept walking—she hadn't forgotten, not at all—hurrying through the university's brick canyons and down the stairs on the far side.

She heard the first flakes against the window just as the fishing report was ending. It was an early, thin snow, but enough to smudge the sun into a diffuse glow beyond the trees. Good riddance she said to it and to the obscene blue sky, to the green bankside and rough beach of Sognsvann—which she couldn't see, of course; the lake was well on the other side of town, clear at the end of the tram line.

She'd gone out just the one time this year, piled into the last car packed tight as a herring tin. For once she didn't mind—the bumping against each other on the turns, everyone with the same destination, was a kind of communion. Then piling off, the cars emptying out, the screams and splashing audible from the platform, the edge of the lake just visible through the trees.

She chose a little flat patch of pebbles beside a small birch thicket from which curls of bark drifted down to her, strips like pencil shavings spiraling through the sunlight, the lighter insides flashing as they fell. She could see the float out in the lake, boys showing off with dives and flips, girls shaking their hair out, eyes scanning to make sure they were being watched. She'd gone to school with some of them, but she didn't call or swim out to join them. They'd been acquaintances through chance. They could choose their friends now.

She rolled her towel up, wrapped it around her head so it was pressed tight against her ears. The boom of belly-flops and cannonballs echoed off the hillside to the east where the trees took over so abruptly, sweeping up in a solid wall to a blunt ridge. There were shrieks and forced laughter, all of it mingling into a wild soundtrack accompanying the pictures flitting across the backs of Mad's eyelids—strange creatures forming from men and animals, women running half-naked through bars of sunlight, the trees moving across the hillside, their trunks rubbing together like crickets' legs.

The sun drew sap and nectar from the trees and

flowers along the shore. She breathed in deeply. Every so often, the sun would be blocked by passing shadows, arms and legs strobing the light. At one point, an especially stubborn shadow entered and lingered. She opened her eyes to see if it was a cloud—and if so how big a cloud and whether it would be followed by more—but instead she saw a boy, maybe thirteen or fourteen, standing over her with his arms crossed on his chest, his hips thrust out. A cocky little bird.

"You're blocking my sun," she said.

The boy took a step to the side. He pointed toward the largest birch in her little grove, the one closest to the shore.

"I'm gonna climb that."

She looked closer. Maybe he was even younger.

"Okay."

"I just wanted to warn you. So you didn't get scared or anything."

Mad managed a smile. "Thanks."

He nodded before hurrying over to the tree and pulling himself up onto the lowest branch. He was a good climber, but she could tell it wasn't as easy as he tried to make out. His progress was deliberate and studied as he passed the long branch overhanging the water she'd assumed he would launch from and continued up the tree. The branches were thinner up above, she could see them bending under him as he climbed.

"Be careful," she said, not quite loud enough for him to hear. He was someone's little brother, and she felt a kind of proxy concern for him. At a crook of branches he stopped and turned to face the water. She shielded her eyes, smiled up at him, proud as if he were her own brother, or maybe her son. Then she noticed his odd smile, and only then saw that he was holding his penis in his hand and waggling it at her.

He let out a strange bird-like noise—meant to be somehow suggestive, she imagined—and she looked away. Off across Sognsvann where the wind had started to roughen the surface like old paper; the clouds had moved in, and the trees crowded closer to the bank.

The branch breaking was almost soundless, but not quite—a little "snick," then he was falling. Sliding down the trunk, branches breaking and scraping across his chest and stomach. He bounced off the big branch, which didn't break, and was thrown flapping into the shallows between two rocks. Mad could see the bone of his left arm jutting out through the skin just below his elbow. He rolled onto his back, wailing.

When she reached him, his little manhood was no more than an exposed stub, flopped to the side and retreating, no longer interested in much of anything. The boy looked up, his eyes wide with pain.

"Goddamn you," he said.

"Excuse me?"

He fumbled his shorts closed with his good hand and hissed up at her: "Fucking bitch!"

The bone of his arm strained against its binding tendons and skin, the ragged break very white in the sun that chose that moment to break through again.

He was a snake in the garden, and she should have done what farmers did, which is lop them in two. Instead she ducked her head, scooped up her towel and her shirt and pants and hurried up the hill toward the tram. Partway up the rocky slope below the station she realized she'd left her sandals behind, but she didn't go back. On the train, with the lake left long behind, she touched the bruises brought up by the pebbles, the pricks and scratches the brush had made on her feet and ankles, taking care to catalog them before they faded.

～

She wished she'd gone back out for the cake. What would it have cost her, really? Her father was disappointed, she knew, even though he tried not to show it. His expectations were so low, but the delivery on them was even poorer. She'd seen the brief hope flash across his face like a fish darting just below the surface, before his tolerant smile erased it as simply as a breeze passing over the water. He could do that; he'd learned how to live in the world. She wondered sometimes if she'd inherited anything more from him than his wide, blunt chin.

She found a couple of half-stale cookies, and they ate those with coffee watching a show about sea turtles. Her father dozed off in the middle, the cookie only nibbled at and fallen onto his chest. She took his plate and saucer and washed them quietly, brushed the crumbs from his sweater, then laid the quilt from Belgium across his legs.

Before she got into bed she made a quick note in the journal she kept on the bedside table:

Hurt no one. Hurt by no one. A blue ribbon day.

She wondered if her father ever read the journal when she was at work. She was afraid it might make him sad if he did, so she added: *All's well on land and sea.* It was something he used to say, something he'd picked up on the ships he worked before the accident. She wasn't sure when he'd stopped saying it.

SOGNSVANN

Just before she fell asleep, the boy at the lake entered her mind once more. His arm was probably healed by now, she guessed. Everything good as new. She imagined taking it and breaking it again, snapping it across her knee like a branch. She thought maybe she could turn this into a ritual, a goodnight story she told herself to feel better, except she didn't feel better. No matter what she did, he healed and aged into confidence and dismissiveness while she stayed where she was, a minor, pitiful character in his story. He would tell it when he got drunk a few years on (she could hear his words slurring, see his red balloon face), describing her unflatteringly—her embarrassment, her scurrying off without her shoes—or sometimes leaving her out altogether. She would become a shadow, a detail among other details he added or dropped depending on his audience. Eventually there wouldn't be anything to prove she'd been there at all, except for the little scar by his elbow where the bone had broken through, an irregular patch shaped like Sognsvann itself that never tanned like the rest of him.

BARN SALE

TWO BOYS GAPE OUT THE clouded back window of a station wagon, their noses swiping across the glass and leaving two slicks like snail tracks. May watches through the knothole in the wall as the car bounces over the rain ruts in the drive, climbing sluggishly past the barn toward the house. A loose strip of plastic trim slaps against the side panel. The car coughs a couple of times, then dies. A tall man with slow eyes climbs out from behind the wheel and stretches lazily. He walks around the car to where three makeshift tables—sheets of plywood resting on sawhorses and fruit crates—hold the scraps of May Aiken's life.

"This must be it," he says.

His wife turns sideways in the passenger seat and scowls at the sagging boards. "Don't we have enough junk of our own?"

"There's treasures at these barn sales sometimes," he says, picking an old rasp up off one of the tables. "Buried old treasures."

The rasp handle is cracked from having been let dry out; when he turns it over, the blade falls out and sticks in the ground.

"Is that one of them?"

He bends down to pick the blade up, sets it back on the table without answering. May watches him touching her things, leaving who knows what all over them. She feels a vague ache in her foot, looks down to see she doesn't have any shoes on. If they see that, she thinks, it'll just be more ammunition.

The two boys climb out through the back window, plop to the ground, and immediately start fighting over an old metal horse. May can see the horse clearly though the kids and the horse are a good twenty yards away—the black curls of its mane and tail, the sweep of neck turned faintly to the left as though it's sniffing something on the air. Her sister left it behind when she moved away, married at seventeen. Her mother took it over then, kept it beside her own bed until the day she died. There are things that keep you tied to the world, May knows, things that have that kind of power.

She presses her eye to the knothole again, blinks twice to bring the little sphere back into focus—brown grass spreading into gray-blue sky—the uniform plainness making it difficult to tell where the ground ends and the sky begins.

"Look what you did," one of the boys yells.

The other boy is holding the horse's left hind leg in his hand, looking down helplessly at the broken edge.

"I didn't. You did."

"Liar!"

"You're the liar!"

"Shut up!" Their mother is out of the car now and planted thickly on the ground. "Both of you."

She stands like a boxer, her feet spread, balanced. A strand of hair has come loose from its metal clip and falls in a slant across her face. She twitches her head sharply and the strand falls back.

The boys fumble with the horse, pressing the leg back into place and letting go, willing it to stay, to heal. But it falls off again, bounces once on the table, and rings against the base of a singed oil lamp. The woman turns back to her husband.

"Your boys," she says.

"Now they're mine."

"It's all right," a voice says from behind them. "No harm done."

May shifts again until she can see Matt standing at the top of the steps, a cup of coffee steaming in one hand and a half-eaten piece of toast in the other.

"We'll pay for it," the woman says, with a hint of resentment.

"Never mind," Matt says. "It was old."

The husband laughs. "That's the idea, isn't it?"

He holds out his hand as Matt comes down the steps. Matt fumbles the piece of toast into his left hand, wipes his right hand on his pant leg, and they shake. The pants are faded just the right amount, with worn patches on the knees and seat that approximate those made by work. Just the way he likes them. Now they're probably stained.

"Lot of stuff," the man says.

"Yes."

"Is it from around here? From on the place?"

"My mother-in-law's, mostly. She grew up here."

Matt glances toward the barn, and May draws back from the knothole. The sound of her own breathing seems impossibly loud as she presses herself against the wall. Back in the depths of the barn something skitters across the planks. She makes a shooing motion with her hands, then knots them up in her sweater again.

The man turns a trivet over in his hand. "Sorry to hear. She passed on, huh?"

"No. No, she's still—with us. It was just getting a little crowded."

"Sure. You don't have to tell me."

At the end of the table, the man's wife is looking at a metal plate partly hidden by a cast iron skillet. She picks it up and turns it over. It's split down the middle, with a hinge on the back and bright silver clasps at either end. A price of $1.25 is marked in felt pen on a small sticker on its underside.

"What's this supposed to be?"

Matt strolls over to where she's standing.

"It says a dollar twenty-five," she says. "For what?"

"You don't have to buy it," her husband says.

"I just want to know what it is they're selling for a dollar twenty-five."

Matt looks at it, turns it over once.

"You'd have to ask my wife."

"If you don't know what it is," the husband says, "you don't need it."

"I'm just asking."

She snatches the plate back and slams it down on the

table. It lets out a ringing that drifts across the yard. The
two boys look up as it passes them. May draws in a quick
breath and holds it. If she goes out there, she knows,
they'll see her and remember. If she stays in the barn
they might forget all about her. But the fixit's out there.

Matt and the others turn to watch as she crosses the
dry yard, ignoring the pops and clicks coming from her
knees and hip and the quick stabs of the dried grass on
the soles of her feet. Matt holds out his hands reflexively,
but she continues on past him, snatches up the plate and
clutches it to her chest.

"What do you think you're doing? These are my
things."

Matt flicks an embarrassed smile toward the man and
woman.

"We've been over this, May. We can't keep it all.
There's no room."

"There's a whole barn."

He looks helplessly at the barn, then down at May,
at her mottled skin beneath the wisps of gun-gray hair.
Then up toward the house, hoping Eve will appear.

"If you've got any questions about anything," he says
at last, "feel free to ask."

"We just did," the woman says.

"Prices are negotiable, of course."

"Sure thing," the man says.

May shuffles backward a few careful steps into the
shade of the walnut tree. The woman watches her, eyes
narrowed. The man takes her by the elbow to turn her
away, but she jerks her arm free and squares up to him.

"Come on, Lee," he says. "Come on. Okay?"

She breathes through her nose. May can see her nostrils widening and narrowing like an animal's. When she finally turns away, May relaxes her grip slightly on the plate. Matt brings a chair over for her. She sits down, sets the plate in her lap and looks at her hand where the metal edge has left a crease in the skin. She opens and closes it, watches the scar fill slowly again with blood.

~

On the little hill behind the house a woodpecker has started working on the fire-hollowed trunk of the oak. A month after her mother died, the tree caught fire in the middle of the night with no lightning or anything else to set it off. It smoldered for almost a week. Kids came from all over the area to watch the big tree turn slowly into a black husk, burning from the inside out. Her daddy kept his own vigil, coming in very late at night for a beer and a meager supper. May would hear him downstairs talking to nobody as he dug through the refrigerator or heated some leftovers on the stove. He was like Loft would be later in the way he saw judgments and trials in misfortune. The fire was another visitation, a further example of god singling him out.

When May came down one of those nights to help him, to keep him from burning the pan or himself, the plate was there on the counter. It shimmered with an otherworldly shine and threw reflected light in miraculous patterns across the walls and ceiling. She picked it up carefully. The clasps were undone and the two halves gaped apart. She pressed them together and fastened the clasps, feeling something pass through her as she clicked them into place. The house gathering itself, a certain heaviness lifting. She wiped some of the soot away and the plate glowed brighter than the fire that had brought it forth.

Her daddy said that somebody had probably stashed it in the tree, one of the McCutcheon kids most likely. She didn't know if he was lying or if he just didn't know any better, but she didn't hold it against him. It was up to her to wield it anyway, she knew that instinctively.

Matt squats beside her and rests his hand on the back of her chair. He won't sit, she knows. Not here, not right on the ground.

"May," he says, but she doesn't look at him.

He sighs and drums his fingers on the back of the chair.

"You know about the barn," he says. "You know it has to come down."

Beyond the fence a new development is going in. Huge houses with little squares of bare land around them. Each with a garage as big as her and Loft's first house, but not a single barn among them.

"You've got no right," she says. "They're my things."

Matt sighs again and stands up. He walks over to a row of old field lugs stacked on the ground and starts unloading them, lining their contents up on the plank tables.

They've kept some things back, but the things they've kept are worthless things that May could have thrown away without a second thought. Books she's already read they think might be worth something someday, knickknacks and china plates. Old pictures, grainy, unrecognizable likenesses of what was supposed to be her—when she was a girl, a newlywed, a mother. Studio pictures with no life in them. The real pictures, the ones

she and her daddy took and developed, are all in the albums in her room. But they're not interested in those,
all they see is empty fields and woods and sky in them—
they can't see the bird hidden in the clump of grass, or
her daddy whistling beside her as she aims the camera.
There's so much they don't understand that she doesn't
know where to start.

A little hand-carved whistle rolls off the table onto
the ground. Loft carved it for Evie when she was just a
little thing. Hair falling into her eyes, her dress dusty and
wrinkled from rolling with the dog in the pasture. She
should have stayed that way, small and sweet and untainted. May laughs to herself. That's one of Loft's words, she
thinks. Untainted. One of his righteous words.

The front door creaks open, and Eve steps out into
the sunlight, shading her eyes with her hand. When she
sees them, she waves and trots down the steps. She comes
to May first and kisses her on the cheek.

"Beautiful day, hmm Mom?" She smells like artificial
flowers. May feels a soreness in her chest. She remembers
a story on the news once about a little girl who fell into
a well. She feels the same thing now, the same tightness.
That clench of something about to slip away. But they
brought that little girl back.

"Morning," Eve says to Matt. Then to both of them:
"How's it going?"

Matt looks at May without saying anything, and
Eve's eyes swivel back to her.

"Mom, are you being good?"

May is looking at her reflection in the plate and
doesn't answer. Eve's shoulders slump.

"Not that thing again."

She tries to take it, and is surprised at her mother's strength.

"Mom, please."

The plate's surface is covered with little dimples that scatter May's features like puzzle pieces shaken out onto a table. She is suddenly terrified of what might happen to the pieces if she lets go. She knows she couldn't collect them all.

Out of the corner of her eye, Eve sees the man and his wife watching them. She lets go of the plate, straightens up and brushes the wrinkles out of her skirt.

"Finding anything?" she says.

"There's some interesting things," the man says. "We're enjoying ourselves."

"Good."

The two boys have found some metal soldiers and are forming them up in skirmish lines in her flower bed. One of them blitzes across a row of pansies and Eve grits her teeth. She looks up at their mother, hoping she'll see Eve's expression and stop them. Instead the woman squints across at May.

"What is that?" she asks.

"Hmm?" Eve says.

"That thing, that plate. Is it something?"

"No. It's nothing."

May laughs. "Nothing."

The woman steps around the table.

"Lee," her husband says, holding up a boot scraper with the bristles worn away. "Look at this." But the woman keeps coming, her legs rubbing against each other with a shrill insect sound. She's still young, May can see, but not for long. Her face is puffed and neglected, the eyes receding back into bruised folds of skin. Her mouth is a red, crooked line like a cut. Her thick shadow falls over May where she sits in the folding chair, wanting suddenly to be up and gone, back in the barn, behind the knothole again.

"What you got there?" she asks, bending close to May's face. "That a prize?"

May forces herself to look at the woman. She notices a small scar beside her left eye and wonders what made it. She touches her own face alongside her eye out of reflex and the woman straightens.

"Cat got your tongue?" she says, and laughs. "Kitty-cat got your tonguey-wung?"

She waits for the others to laugh too.

"It's a fixit," May says at last.

"Oh god," Eve says.

"A what?"

"A fixit."

The woman blinks down at her.

"What's a fixit when it's at home?"

"Just what it says."

"What, like a doctor or a repairman or something?"

May laughs. "No."

The woman points toward the station wagon with a finger girdled with yellow stains. "Can it fix that old piece of junk?"

"It won't help you," May says, pulling the plate closer. "Go away."

The woman tenses. Her husband shuffles over and touches her arm lightly.

"Lee," he says, but she doesn't seem to notice him.

"Why not?" she snarls down at May. "There something wrong with me?"

May holds the plate out toward her so she can see her reflection. The woman's face fills with a sudden, bursting red.

"You're a rude old woman. You're a crazy old bitch!"

Matt steps between them and holds out his hand.

"Thanks for coming up," he says. "Sorry you couldn't find anything."

The woman glares past him at May. Her husband reaches his hand carefully around and shakes Matt's hesitantly.

"Thanks for the look-see. There's some interesting things." His smile is tight and close to breaking. He touches his wife's shoulder.

"Come on, Lee."

"I want that," she says, pointing to the plate. "We've got a dollar twenty-five, don't we? We aren't that broke."

"You don't want that."

"Don't tell me what I want."

May grips the plate tighter. Eve looks at her, then back at the woman.

"We said it was for sale, so it's for sale," she says.

The woman slaps her husband on the chest.

"Give me the money."

"Can't you forget it?"

Her hand remains extended, unwavering. May looks closely at Eve. She's tried to tell her before, but she doesn't understand.

"It's got powers," May says.

"Stop it."

"It kept all this here. It kept us together."

"Are you kidding? Who, Mom? They're all gone—

James, Dad. It didn't fix them."

"That's not how it works, you know that."

Eve's hand shoots out suddenly and snatches the plate away.

"No, I don't know. I never have known. As far as I can tell, it's done just the opposite."

"Don't say that."

"Why not? Come on then, let's see some magic. Bring James back, how about that?" She looks around theatrically, her free arm slashing the air. "Where is he? Why isn't he here?"

May looks involuntarily toward the railroad crossing out of sight beyond the trees. It was abandoned some time ago; the trains don't use that track anymore.

"He was too broken, Evie."

Eve's teeth clench, the lines of her cheeks showing sharp as knife edges.

"This is going to stop."

The man has the money out, his hand extended uncertainly. The bill is crumpled and dirty, the green ink almost black. The quarter, in contrast, gleams from frequent rubbing. Eve reaches for the money, but Matt steps forward and bats the man's hand away. The bill flutters to the ground. The quarter sails high and spins against the sun, flashing on and off, off and on.

"Let her keep it," Matt says. "For god's sake, what difference does it make?"

The quarter whirls and flashes. It has broken free of the earth and won't ever come down.

~

May didn't understand herself at first how it worked,

when she gave it that silly name—but she was just a little girl. She thought it was like some kind of magic glue, that it could heal all things sundered. She tried it on broken toys, a gash on her leg, even on a dead magpie, but she saw it couldn't put things back once they'd come apart. All it could do was hold them where they were for a little while, keep them from flying all the way apart. Maybe not forever, but for a little while. It was like the chemical she and her daddy used after a picture was developed in the little darkroom off the kitchen. That's where she got the name, from a bottle in there. It fixed things like that, in time. Folded open—kept open—it slowed life just enough to catch up.

Loft didn't believe any of it, of course, he thought it was a kind of blasphemy even. He waved it in her face one day, the air singing off it and the light bending.

"See there," he said, "right there? That says *Mexico*. You think God's gonna put *Mexico* on one of his creations?"

"He did on Mexico."

"Damn it, May."

"I never said it was God."

"Well who then?"

"I don't know."

And she didn't. But it wasn't any harder to believe for that. Maybe it worked off her dreams, or the light running through the farm and the woods, she didn't know. And she didn't care. It gave back to her the same as she gave to it.

She heard Loft flip the clasps before she could stop him, turned to see him clapping the halves together.

"Look," he said, holding it up. "A silver taco."

132

He laughed, while May stood there—her heart broken—watching her husband and their life together hurtle away.

~

At the barn, the man has to turn around. He carves a clumsy Y, and at the leg of the Y he backs the station wagon hard into the corner. A length of siding hangs in the bumper. He lays on the gas until the board finally snaps, a ragged piece still wedged against the taillight.

He steps out of the car, stares down at the deep V in his bumper, at the splintered red board jutting out, pointing like a finger. With some effort, he finally frees the board, holds it up helplessly. He starts toward Matt, holding the board like a dead pet, but Matt waves him off. He hesitates, then leans the board against the side of the barn. He shrugs an apology and gets back in his car. In the passenger seat, his wife glares at the barn, then at Matt, then at May. They have all conspired, she knows.

When the car's dust trail finally dissipates, Eve goes into the house. She comes out a moment later with a suitcase and sets it down by the car. She goes back in and comes out with another one. Matt has given the plate back to May. She holds onto it tightly, rocking slowly in the lawn chair.

"Are you going to help?" Eve calls.

Matt looks briefly at May, then turns away and goes into the house.

~

When May and Loft first moved back into her daddy's house, she'd take the fixit out sometimes and study its shifting surface while Loft listened to his television preachers scolding him like a child. Downstairs James and Evie played their music and laughed at jokes she didn't understand, their quick lives a secret from her already. Later, at dinner, they would be briefly a family before the kids dumped their dishes in the sink and darted off. When they made it back every night from wherever it was they went, it was another little miracle she credited to the fixit.

It drove Loft crazy. At least until later, when he started to lose track and began believing in even wilder things. When he heard the voice of God coming from the television, and May would find him staring rapt at the screen while Vanna White turned the letters over, holding his breath, thinking the answers to his deepest questions were about to be spelled out for him. Puzzling over the words and phrases for hours afterward, repeating them out loud until they were just sounds, getting angrier as meaning drifted farther and farther away.

When the shows were all over and the sun was long gone he'd kneel by the bed and say his prayers like a little boy. Once in a while he'd try to coax May down there with him.

"It troubles me that you don't believe," he'd say. "I worry about you."

She never understood what he meant. How he could think she didn't believe.

"Time to go, Mom," Eve says.

May can tell without looking at her that she's been crying. She suspects it's her job to comfort her, but she doesn't feel inclined at the moment.

"I know you'll like it," Eve says. "You'll make friends."

"I had friends already," May says. She can't bring herself to look at her daughter, at the blunt woman's face that swallowed the child.

After a moment, Eve draws her hand away.

May is alone then, and she doesn't mind it so much. She sits in the chair and listens to the grasshoppers clicking in the grass, the faint wind up in the walnut rattling the leaves and making the branches creak like rusty machinery. There are possibly the voices of people mixed in, too, people she'd known, but she can't be sure. She thinks she hears her mother and Loft arguing—which is impossible, since her mother died long before Loft came along. A squirrel starts up in the tree and James enters quietly, as he always did. She tries to push him out, but he won't go. He's the troublemaker again, standing in the doorway at the far end of her room snapping the fixit open and closed. Mocking her. He winks at her and she slams her eyes shut. When she opens them again, he's gone and there's just a faint impression where he was, like a wind matting down the grass.

～

Her thoughts aren't as clear as they once were, she knows that, and it troubles her. The edges of things have lost some of their distinction, and she's not as sure of herself. She wonders if her ideas about the fixit and its powers have always been there, or if it's something new, a drift into foolishness like Loft seeing God on the Wheel of Fortune. Time does seem sometimes to be loosing its grip on her.

Matt leans against the loaded van, raises his hand in a tired wave. May waves back, then takes the plate in one hand and with the other pushes herself up from the chair. She rocks a little on her feet; the massive spread of the walnut dwarfs her, makes her lose herself for a moment. She takes three short steps, four, lets her meager weight gather, lifts her feet higher and starts to run. Her knees pump, the tendons and ligaments creaking inside her like an old harness. She can feel time tugging against her like a fish ticking the drag as she runs through the open barn door, past the workbench and the tack room, and on into the black body of the barn.

The darkness closes in around her, brushes up against her. She stands still and listens for sounds of pursuit, but there's only her own strained breathing and the hiss of blood in her ears. Maybe they won't follow her. They're afraid, she knows, of so many things. Then the car door slams and they begin calling, like children at the end of a game.

She clutches the fixit to her chest, rubbing it in quick circles. She feels heat rising from it, hears its hum like far-off starlings. The barn begins to groan around her. Old cans filled with bolts and washers rattle on the shelves. A cloud of hay chaff descends to her, glittering like gold dust.

Far back in the barn, a hinge squeaks, and a line of light stretches out beside her. She follows it back through old shadows and bits of chewed leather to the muck-out chute she'd forgotten all about, a low door in the back wall that Loft had nailed shut years ago. She has to crawl to get through it, like she did when she was little. The ground is soft with dried manure that's been ground to dust, the smell familiar and purposeful.

As she starts up the little hill behind the house, the

barn collapses on itself like a paper foldout. The walls fall away, the roof hangs in the air for a moment, then splits in two and flutters to the ground. It all happens in silence, the noise only coming after, rushing into the vacuum left by the barn's absence. She is halfway up the hill by then and feels the wind from it, but she doesn't turn around to look. Loft's wife, she thinks, and laughs. Gone to salt.

Down below, Matt and Eve rush to the wreckage of the barn and begin throwing boards aside, calling her name. She should wave or yell back, she knows, let them know she's all right, but she doesn't. She brushes a film of dust from the plate and buffs the pale metal with the sleeve of her dress. Her face is multiplied many times across its surface—her tiny, wrinkled mouth, her eyes like olive pits. She takes a stray bundle of hair between her fingers and tucks it behind her ear, then climbs the rest of the way to the top of the hill. She undoes the two clasps and gently folds the plate closed. There is a sound like a string breaking, quiet and very far off.

She sets the plate at the base of the burnt oak and takes a step back, laces her fingers the way she'd seen Loft do and whispers a little prayer in his honor:

"I'd like to buy a vowel."

Then she continues on down the other side of the hill toward the creek and the last remaining pasture. There's no rush. It's a lovely day—the end of summer, not unbearably hot. It's the kind of day that, in her time, they would have sooner died than waste.

MASTERPIECE

DAN DISLIKED DOGS, HE ALWAYS had, but that wasn't why Nora went out and got one. She bought the dog because she wanted to reconstruct some part of their old world, the one they'd lived in when they were kids. The current one wasn't working, it was a blown experiment. They hardly talked anymore, and when they did it was Dan criticizing her, berating her for nothing. It was frustrating. So she bought the puppy—the puppy would be Dan, down even to the red hair, an obedient little thing following her around without question or objection, content in believing that each word and gesture of hers was an act of god. It was a good plan. But as it turned out, Paramus was as big a letdown as Dan.

To begin with, the name. She'd thought it was something classical, a Greek god or a philosopher. She couldn't remember where she'd heard it, maybe PBS. Of course it was Dan who pointed out—smirking as he seemed to always be doing these days—that Paramus was a town in New Jersey. By then it was too late; the name was in the vet's book beside the chip code and the heartworm prescription. Set in stone. If he got lost and someone found him, took him in and had him scanned, they would see the name and they'd laugh too. At her. Her ridiculous attempt at erudition. Where, she wondered sometimes, did it end?

At the moment, Paramus was digging in the garden. She thumbed the hose and sprayed him with water that was sure to be freezing. She felt a twinge of sympathy. Then she saw his muddy muzzle and the uprooted eggplant, and it passed. The garden was struggling. Her one boastable talent and it was failing her.

"You planted too late," Dan had said.

"What do you know about it?"

"I know a screw-up when I see one."

She lifted her foam kneeler, scooted up along the row of eggplants. They'd be eating a lot of eggplant. She dug at the nutgrass, pulling each clump up carefully to make sure she got all the roots. She imagined each one screaming a little as she slowly extracted it, and drew the process out, smiling to herself. There was nothing disturbing about that, she assured herself. She was the garden's guardian, it was her duty. Things were always horning their way in; she had to be vigilant.

She smushed a pill bug under her trowel and thought about the episode coming up this Sunday on PBS, a new show, a new female detective. One of those British ladies with their better-tended gardens. She loved those shows. They were the reason she still kept a TV. It had been a nuisance to change over to digital—the little box and antenna, the terminology like a foreign language—but it had been worth it for those little old ladies. The Pembrokes and Duchesses and Marples.

Paramus barked in the side yard and clawed at the gate. Nora straightened up with difficulty and leaned out to see what the commotion was. Too early for the mail-man—the lazy mailman with the lazy eye—but there was definitely someone there. She could see his shoes in the gap beneath the gate.

A rapist? Not in broad daylight, surely. That would be too much. But then again, who knew these days? Everyone was so bold and pushy. The Keller boys down the street sold pot right out in the open. They flipped her the bird once when she watched their transaction for too long. She just wanted to let them know that she knew, she didn't care about the pot. She'd had a joint or two herself in her day—did they still call them that, joints? They must have new words by now, a fresh vocabulary to separate them from their parents with their tie-dyed shirts and Grateful Dead stickers on their SUVs. Really, a time came when—

The rapist or Mormon or whatever was peering over the gate, a tall man with thick blond hair and dark eye-brows.

"I'm looking for Dan," he said.

She struggled to her feet—first to one haunch, then up onto a heel, wobbling like a poorly made toy. Then one last push and . . . up. She brushed the nutgrass and dirt from her apron and crossed the yard at a calm, even pace so as not to appear either too anxious or too apprehen-sive. The man had been standing on his toes, apparently.

He lowered himself now so that all she could see was a little bit of a blond cowlick. How cute, she thought, wanting to lick her palm and mat it down.

The gate always hung up on the concrete cauliflowered around the base of the post. She'd asked Dan to fix it several times, she wasn't sure why—he wouldn't have had any idea how to go about it. It was her kind of chore, as most things were. She pulled on the gate, and at the same time the visitor pushed from his side. When the ends of the boards cleared the concrete, the gate flew open; it would have knocked her down if she wasn't ready for it. The visitor meanwhile hurtled through, and just managed to catch himself before plowing into her. He came to a stop with his chest touching lightly against hers, their knees bumping. None of it painful, not at all. Just a bit awkward.

"Sorry," she said.

"My fault."

His clothes were tidy and pressed-looking. He was almost certainly a new boyfriend of Dan's, or whatever they were meant to be called. Dan had corrected her terminology a number of times, but not with enough consistency that she could be sure of herself. In any case, they came and went so quickly that she never had time to offend them.

"Dan's not home. You're welcome to wait."

She cleared off the glider—brushed away the leaves, smacked the cushions a couple of times. There was nowhere else, really. She certainly didn't want him going inside the house.

"All right," he said. "Thanks."

Paramus sniffed at the his ankles, then scurried off to

pee on the brown fringe of the lawn.

"Can I get you a biscuit?" she asked.

"A what?"

"Sorry, a cookie or something?"

"No thanks. I'm good."

A number of responses presented themselves, but thankfully they all stayed inside, rattling around among the crates and steamer trunks piled in the corners of her brain. What a clutter it was up there! She shook her head. A little hair fell loose; she tucked it back into place.

"You like gardening?" the man asked.

"I do."

"You must have a green thumb."

She paused, took a breath, pushed a mental armoire back against the wall.

"It's at a sort of in-between stage right now."

"No, it looks nice. Well-tended."

She was proud for a moment, but only a moment, before a troubling image presented itself of her smiling into the camera at JC Penney, her green thumb raised, surrounded by a loving family of carrots and zucchini.

"It's not all I do," she said.

"I'm sure it isn't."

"Really."

"I believe you," he said, laughing and lifting a stray strand of hair from his forehead with two long fingers.

She'd never really understood laughter, the pleasure of it. If it was aimless, harmless—okay, maybe. But it never was, it was always leveled squarely at her. Once in a while at Dan, but he never seemed to notice or to mind.

"Something to drink," she said.

Not a question, so no need to wait for an answer.

Working around the dishes and seedlings in the sink,
she plopped a can of lemonade into a pitcher and buried
the can deep in the garbage. Beneath a bag of onions she
found a shriveled lemon, cut it open and squirted a few
seeds into the pitcher. As she passed back through the
house, she saw the shabby rooms through his eyes—the
unremarkable home of unremarkable people. She'd definitely keep him outside.

She set the pitcher on the little table, along with the
small tray and glasses she carried like a waitress in her
other hand.

"Wow, lemonade? You didn't have to do that."

"It's no problem," she said. "It's that time of day."

She had no idea what that meant, but he smiled so
she let it stand. What an unusual day it was turning out
to be! Her visitor sipped his lemonade. She poured herself a glass and sipped it too, slurping a little around the
ice cubes.

He smiled again. It was a very nice smile.

"Will your guy be here soon?" he asked.

"My . . . ?"

"I mean, if you have one."

What in the world was he getting at, some kind of
orgy? He didn't seem the type, but who could tell.

"I'm single."

He looked at her blankly for a moment, until a light
went on. He set the glass down awkwardly on the table,
and a little lemonade sloshed over the side.

"Sorry, I didn't mean that."

She recognized his discomfort and felt a stirring
camaraderie.

"It's not your fault. Dan likes to do this, put people in uncomfortable situations."

"That's not very nice."

"You get used to it. He's been doing it since we were kids—setting up little ambushes, catching me off guard. I'm sure there's a term for it, but I don't know what it is. Something pathological."

He laughed, and it wasn't so bad this time. They sipped their lemonade. The sun fell in bands through the pecan leaves onto the table, onto her hands and across his suit jacket. She could smell the fresh-turned soil in the garden.

Then Dan was there in the doorway, one foot pushing the slider aside.

"What a pretty little scene! Cinderella and Prince Charming."

She tried to think if it was Cinderella or Sleeping Beauty who'd married Prince Charming. She knew if she asked which it was—or, worse, corrected him—he'd find some way to mock her with it.

"You haven't talked to her," their visitor said.

Dan clicked his tongue and sat on the glider, patted him on the leg.

"You've been gossiping."

"We've been having a nice time," Nora said.

"No one has a nice time with a lawyer."

"Well I did."

Dan picked up one of the lemonade glasses and ran it across his forehead. Like Vivien Leigh or someone.

"They are paid to charm," he said. "Like hookers."

He was in full brat mode, the jealous little boy again. Nora was tempted to call him out on it right there, but what would their guest think? Victim and tormentor would change places, just like that. So instead, she yanked the glass from his hand, clattered it onto the tray with hers.

"Don't hurry off on my account, Cinder."

Their visitor fidgeted.

"Dan," he said, scolding.

"Oh don't worry about her, Steven. She's tougher than both of us."

Which was true. Or used to be.

~

Dan was crying again. Dan was always crying. He wanted his mother, but his mother was gone. There was only Nora. He didn't seem to consider that she might want her mother too.

"He's a complainer, isn't he?" Dad said.

"I don't know what he wants."

"Nobody does."

Dad drank the glass of water she'd brought to wash down his heart medicine.

"He's a sensitive boy. That doesn't worry me so much. But the sensitive ones, when they make it through . . . they can turn hard later."

He handed the empty glass back to Nora and turned the band saw on again to drown Dan out, cocooning himself in sawdust and noise. Well, who could blame him? He was in over his head.

She made some chocolate milk for Dan. Thirteen and still drinking chocolate milk. He took it from her without looking up.

"Those assholes," he said between gulped sobs.

"I know."

"Fucking Neanderthals!"

"You're better than them. They'll see it eventually."

"But when? I can't do this forever."

"High school will be different."

Of course she knew it wouldn't be; or if it was, it would only be worse. Dan wasn't looking for truth from her, she knew that. He didn't want anything to do with it.

"I'll take you tomorrow," she said.

"Could you?"

"Sure."

He settled down eventually, went soft and rubbery in front of the TV. She made dinner and they all ate in the living room. Nobody spoke, except on the screen, sitcom families making it through their hilarious, enviable problems.

Before she went to bed, she stood in front of the mirror in just her underwear. She couldn't see her head, the mirror was too short. She was like a grotesque beheaded statue. She swelled out along the sides too, overflowing the edges. Dan laughed sometimes, on his meaner days, at how she couldn't fit in the mirror. If it was a door, he said, she'd get stuck.

But it wasn't a door, despite what all those childhood books had implied. There was no way from here into some bright, enchanted world. She looked at her rounded football shoulders, the rolls drooping over her hips. Even if it was a door, what good would that do? Wherever you went, you had to take you along.

She could smell herself under the covers. Thick and moldy like the garden. She slid her hand under the band of her panties, ran her finger roughly along the turned furrow, and fell asleep to the sound of her own blubbering.

The next day she pushed two eighth graders into the fence so hard the chain link left diamond impressions on their faces. They'd leave Dan alone for a little while, but it was only a temporary fix. She knew that, even if it never seemed to get through to Dan. He stood behind her the whole time laughing that thin, cutting laugh that struck her as something feral, the chittering of a weak animal hidden safely somewhere while the real animals went about their hard business.

The two boys bounced like Raggedy Andys from the fence, but they didn't cry. Even under their fear, she could see their scorn and hate, could hear the jokes at her expense waiting to be made at lunch.

"Who's the faggot now?" she growled. "Who's the faggot now?"

It was rhetorical; neither one answered. They just bounced and bounced and waited for it to be over with.

~

"We're too old to be living like this," Dan said. "The two of us in this place. We're not kids anymore."

Nora had been trying for some time to put her finger on when he'd changed, when he'd turned from a puppy into a nasty, snarling dog. Standing at the edge of the garden with the sting of sweat working into her cracked hands, the possibility occurred to her that he *hadn't* changed, that that was the problem—neither of them had.

"What, are you going to move in with Steven?" she said.

Dan sniffed, his chin against his chest. "A little too soon for that."

Nora watched him closely. Was he going to cry now, or turn on her again?

"I feel like I'm floating out on the ocean or something," he said, "and the land's getting farther and farther away."

"I've never seen you go in the ocean. You hardly go in the pool."

"It's a metaphor, goddammit."

"Well it's a stupid one, it's got nothing to do with you."

"God!"

He flopped onto the glider and pushed it into motion. His arms were crossed now, his chin still tucked in. She tried to ignore him, the angry squeak of the glider and his breath whistling out of his nose in counterpoint. Every time they tried to get somewhere, they ended up here. Stuck. It would be up to her, of course, to get them unstuck.

"I can ask around," she said. "I might be able to find a place. I know a couple of people."

The glider squeaked to a stop.

"Really?"

"Sure. Probably."

She went back to digging.

"Nora." Softer now.

She didn't turn around, she didn't want to look at him right then. Knowing, maybe, that he'd be smiling.

~

Dad was in the garage as usual when he died, crumpled

to the floor of his shop with the table saw still running. He'd been working on what he called his Masterpiece for as long as Nora could remember. It filled most of the garage, pushing everything else aside.

"We have to finish it," Nora said, Dad in his urn on the driveway beside her.

"How?" Dan said. "What even is it?"

"It's his Masterpiece."

"Well yeah. But what's it supposed to be?"

Nora studied it, its underlying skeleton of 1x4s overlaid with roughly bent panels of plywood. Parallel channels disappeared into the far shadows of the garage, branching wildly and unpredictably. Arms spiraled up into the rafters and in between the legs of castoff furniture exiled here by their mother. You could see the calendar of their childhood in the wood—from the newer, pale pine closest to them, back through wasted months and years to the first gray, dimpled planks sagging by the side door. His life—and theirs—laid out.

"Jesus Christ," Dan said. "What a joke."

She slapped him for the first and only time in their lives, hard. The slap echoed in the shop.

"He had something in mind. It would have been amazing," she said.

Dan whimpered and kicked a strut out from underneath the structure, causing a four-foot section to sink down onto its knees. Nora let him be this time. He ran up to his room and stayed there for the last two days of vacation before heading back for his final year of college. She suspected he never really got over the slap, that it was the gestating act of the paperwork sitting inside the house right now waiting for her signature. His slow-cooked revenge.

After he'd left, she followed the line of ramps and troughs through the shop, studied its joints and angles. At one point, as she leaned into a chute, she saw her name lightly carved into the wood. NORA in jagged capitals, nothing more. He'd been thinking of her at least, at one point. Was she supposed to understand something just by seeing her name here, carved by his hand?

She dug through the workbench drawers and inside the tool chest for the master plan she was sure existed. A set of blueprints, diagrams detailing the thing's function and ultimate shape. But all she could find was a secreted pack of Marlboros and a couple of *Playboy*s from the 1980s. A quaint collection. No key to his vision in full flower. She decided she'd never know; it was like trying to piece a dinosaur together from a single bone.

It was dark when she left the shop and closed the door behind her. She hadn't gone in again until now, almost ten years later. It looked even more forlorn, with the door open and sunlight playing along the new cracks and the black patches of mold on the undersides. She found her name, ran her fingers across the letters. She closed her eyes to see if she'd be able to make it out if she was blind, or if it would just be gibberish.

Poor Dad, she thought. But she wished he'd helped her along a little more.

～

She planted her hands on either side of the sink, little sparks going off just under her scalp. She took down the tin cup she kept on a nail by the window and filled it with tap water. It tasted like rust, but she drank it anyway.

Out on the glider, Dan and Steven leaned close together. Steven pulled a folded paper out of his pocket like a magician and set it in Dan's hand. Dan kissed him again and laid the paper between them.

She reached across the counter and cranked the window partway open, breathed in a big lungful of air. Steven and Dan were laughing—well, Dan was. Steven was only smiling, a halfhearted smile she was familiar with, the kind you fight to hang on to against a steadily creeping discomfort.

"Don't be so dramatic," Dan was saying. "It's what she needs."

The smile was struggling harder.

"There are other ways, you know. Like talking."

"Nah, that never works."

"It does for most people."

"Nora's not most people. She's like a St. Bernard—you have to rub her tummy and let her take the medicine on her own."

It wasn't out of character for Dan, or even especially hurtful, compared to other things he'd said over the years. But it shattered the afternoon nonetheless. She saw fairies and unicorns falling from the shimmering sky, a dung-spattered pig rooting through her garden.

She blinked and swallowed. She tasted the metal of the cup on her lip, felt it on her teeth. It was all so coincidental, she and Dan being related. The fact was they'd been thrown together like survivors from some distant wreck, bickering ever since across a floundering raft without once giving thought to what sank the ship in the first place.

When she didn't come back out, Steven came looking for her. Wearing the same half-assed smile, which re-treated for good when the tin cup glanced off his shoulder and slammed into the wall, leaving a misshapen stain on his jacket. He gawked at it with a dismay that had no legitimate business there.

~

All sorts of plants were poisonous in some respect, could be ground or baked or mixed for a little surprise for little brother. She had a book inside the house listing all the effects, accompanied by sketches of cartoon people in various degrees of distress. She pulled a dandelion up by the roots and tossed it onto the pile.

"It was your idea," Dan said.

"I've changed my mind."

"Of course you have. As usual."

"What?"

"You make the decisions, you call the shots. What do you think that's like for me?"

"I have no idea."

"No, you don't. It's you and dad still. The son he never had."

She sank the trowel deeper into the soil, pressed as hard as she could until it was halfway in to the handle. Then she gave it a sharp twist. She imagined something snapping, a neck or a leg.

"If you had a job—" Dan was saying behind her.

She turned and wiped her hands on her apron. Stood and set them on her hips, elbows out and sharp.

"I have a job."

He looked past her at the garden. "That's not a job. That's a hobby."

But, of course, it wasn't the garden she meant. Dan was the job, as he always had been.

"It's my house too."

"Look, it's only reasonable that the worker gets the say."

"You sound like a communist."

"Please."

"You're the red menace."

"Jesus," blowing the persimmon hair from his eyes in exaggerated exasperation. "You and your hilarious hyperbole."

Did it bother him that he was such a cliché? Probably not. This parody was an easy role; being him was a little too fraught.

"It's not like I'm turning you out on the street. You can get a nice apartment for what I'm giving you."

"What you're giving me?"

"Yes."

"It's not yours to give."

He pulled the paper out of his pocket as if it pained him. As if it was the last thing in the world he wanted to do.

"It's time, Nor."

Paramus was sniffing the cuffs of his slacks. Nora hoped he'd lift a leg and let loose. Dan pushed him away roughly, almost kicking him.

"Don't do that," she said.

"Train him then. Teach him some manners."

"I could do you both at the same time."

He let out another little exhausted sigh.

"We'll talk when you're reasonable. I didn't think you'd take it like this."

"Then you don't know me."

"I guess not."

"You really should by now."

The demure horn of Steven's Prius peeped out front. She took the paper and tossed it on the ground by the cucumbers. **QUIT CLAIM** in bold letters, like an advertisement for something nobody wanted.

"I suppose you're going to dump your boyfriend when he's done screwing me."

"Screwing you?" Dan tittered, turning away. "Dream on."

After he left, she sank down next to the rose bush's twisted trunk. Dan didn't know it, but she'd buried a handful of Dad's ashes underneath. To have him nearby, she reasoned to herself, for advice and support. She knew it was ridiculous; Dad had never been much use for either.

The day shuffled like a vagrant toward evening. A thorn pressed into her knee, but she didn't move. At the far end of the garden, Paramus tore an Anaheim chile loose and tossed it into the air.

～

Maybe it was her fault; she'd turned him into this. She should have let the mean world have him. Now she didn't know how to defend herself, only him.

He came and went, spending all his time with Steven, waiting her out. Well, she could wait too.

"If I had your patience," Dad had said once. "You'd still have a mother."

Which wasn't true, of course. He blamed himself, but their mother hadn't left because of anything he'd done. It just wasn't the life she wanted, being a mother out in the farthest of the suburbs. She read magazines like *Harper's* and *The Atlantic*, and something called *Barking Muse*—an artist in search of an art. She never found it, as far as Nora knew. She ended up in another suburb a little closer to the city, a little less provincial, but not so different. Nora visited her once, and that was enough.

"She would have made us all miserable," Nora said.

Dad started to object, to defend her, but what was the point? Nora had been there, she'd seen them all falling lower and lower in her esteem. They were strangers in the end, people she might have nodded to on the street, or might just as easily have walked right past.

"Anyway, she couldn't cook for shit," Nora added.

"Don't say 'shit.'"

"She couldn't."

"No," Dad said. "She was a terrible cook."

Nora, on the other hand, was an excellent one. Especially with her own vegetables, the beautiful tomatoes and beets and cucumbers she coaxed from the depleted ground. She never used a cookbook, she knew what went together, what worked without anyone having to teach her. The doctor told her once that Dad had probably lived ten years longer because of her cooking. She doubted that, but it was nice to hear. What happiness could top that?

She spilled a little wine on the papers, pushed them to the side of the cutting board. She'd picked some carrots earlier in the day, and now a little water was dripping from the greens, mixing with the wine and wicking up into the sheaf of documents. Steven had dropped off a fresh copy the day before—something new had been added, she hadn't paid attention to what—and told her he felt bad about the whole thing.

"It's your job."

"Yeah, but still."

"Don't worry. It'll work out."

The front door slammed, and she heard Dan slump into the sprung armchair by the fireplace they used now as a magazine dump. They hadn't lit a fire in it since Dad passed.

"He's leaving me."

"Who?"

"Who do you think?"

"Oh."

"He says I'm heartless."

"It's just a fight. It won't last."

She washed the dirt from the carrots and started to peel them. What an invention, the peeler! So simple and perfect, the way it stripped the rough outer layer off so cleanly, curling it like a party ribbon. She hated to throw the peelings away, even into the compost. Something beautiful should be done with them—the carrot underneath was utilitarian and nourishing; the beauty was in the peel.

"Do you think I'm heartless?" Dan asked.

She began arranging the pieces on a paper towel, finding a natural pattern in the disorder. Or, more accurately, appreciating their natural disorder's beauty.

"You do! Jesus."

He jumped up and started pacing behind her, back and forth across the loose board by the pantry that creaked in an oddly soothing, familiar rhythm.

"You can be a little cold," she said.

"What the hell do you know? Look at you—what a piece of work!"

"That's right. I'm a goddamn masterpiece."

The creaking stopped. He tried to laugh, but it was a failure. She looked at his face, red and indrawn, saw that indeed it wasn't a child's anymore. The frown lines slashing down on either side of his nose were like their mother's. Nora didn't know why that should surprise her, but it did.

Dan started pacing again, treading each time over the loose floorboard. Dad had spent a whole weekend once trying to fix it.

"What bullshit!"

She wondered what note it was, the creak. Maybe she could locate it on the piano, give a name to it.

"I poured my heart out!" Dan continued. "What in god's name does everyone want from me?"

She let him go on like that, he'd get tired eventually. Tomorrow he'd pout, but that would end too. And she'd sign the papers. What was there here anymore, really, to hold on to? Habit, that's all.

She'd find a place closer to town, or farther away. Something had to give if she didn't want to end up like Dad, with a pile of sticks tacked together that did nothing and went nowhere. In her case, of course, it would be the garden. Rows and rows of weedy, thin vegetables dribbling off into briars and piles of compost.

She looked out the kitchen window at the rose bush stunted with over-tending, at the squash vines creeping already toward the garage wall, all roots and runners.

"What was I thinking?" she said, very quietly.

Dan cursed and threw a pewter tankard to the floor.

It bounced just in front of Paramus, who dribbled a little pee on the floor.

Poor little thing, all lost and helpless. Who was going to watch over him now?

The dog, of course, she'd take with her.

THE SHALLOW END

THE FIRST TIME HE SAW the eye in the back fence, he thought it was just a peculiarity of paint swirled on a knot. The fence was dimpled and pitted, with multiple coats of paint peeling independently, an abstract canvas across which images often appeared transiently, morphing or disappearing when Ludlow looked too closely or away. The eye, though, winked. That was a first.

He winked back.

After a week or so of this—as can happen—the strange became the ordinary. He and the eye would acknowledge each other and go about their morning business, Ludlow scraping out songs on his half-tuned Yamaha or just watching the sky drag past above the pecan tree. The eye observed, or pulled away and left a hole behind, with sometimes a pair of legs scissoring up toward the back door of the house he could see just the corner

159

of. It was always gone by lunch time when he sat down at the little living room table across from the picture of his daughter propped up in its silver frame with a seashell in each corner.

"I suspect someone's attached to it," he said.

He knew the picture couldn't answer back, but it didn't hurt anyone to pretend. To try to imagine what Jeannie might say in a given situation.

"A child's my guess," for instance.

"A girl, I think."

"Does she say anything?"

"No. Not a thing."

"Shyness can be overpowering."

He smiled at the picture. The young often had a wisdom we'd long let go of.

In the afternoon, he generally fed the fish. Sitting on the diving board, he'd dribble a handful of pellets into the sluggish pool at the deep end. Sometimes he'd see the fish's back, mottled white and orange like a burn victim, but generally all that showed was a ring spreading out where its mouth broke the surface and sucked the food in.

"You can feed it if you want," he said to the eye, which often returned around that time. It blinked once and vanished. He heard the screen door squeak open and glide quietly closed. Unlike his, which always slapped loudly, banging twice before settling uneasily into its warped frame.

"The bottom of the sea is so near," he sang, "your face I can see so clear."

The fish rose with a slurping sound, rippling the carpet of algae.

He never drank on open mic night, even though the drinks and beers were half-price for performers. He'd seen people fall off their stools on stage and launch into obscene tirades; he needed his wits about him. He lost his place so easily as it was—even though they were his own songs—when he looked out and saw all those faces looking up at him.

People had started recording him lately on their phones, so he was making an impression. The applause had gotten more raucous too—and the laughter, but that was just the liquor. The feeling that he was finally connecting was deeply satisfying. He found it hard to wipe the smile off his face when he was up there.

"What are you playing tonight?" somebody asked while he was waiting to go on.

"Something new," he said.

He half-recognized him; a poet, he thought. He wore a wool scarf wrapped twice around his neck even though outside the last of the sun was glaring off the blacktop and a little twister of dust was whirling by.

"If it's anything like 'Sobbing for Apples,'" the poet said, "it'll be a hit."

Ludlow smiled and thanked him. He didn't really like talking before a show, it broke his concentration. But mutual support was the thing here. Everybody leaned on everybody else, like trees in a forest. He took out his notebook, jotted that down.

During the chorus of "Friday Night Fights" he dropped his pick, which broke the mood a little. He could hear it rattling around inside the guitar, sliding from side to side as he tilted the body and shook it. They cut him short after that, which was a little disappointing. But he got a big hand anyway.

The sun dragged him out of bed the next day, too warm and too bright. He ate breakfast with sunglasses on, going through two bowls of cereal, three fried eggs, and a peanut butter and jelly sandwich. There was a strange kind of void down around his stomach—like hunger, but not quite—that skittered out of the way whenever he tried to pinpoint it. He swallowed, tried to force a burp, but nothing came up. He squeezed his arms around his chest and felt a little quiver just under the skin—a squirrel inside the walls, sprinting around and over studs, clawing up the insulation.

He looked for the eye in the fence, but it wasn't there. He put his own eye to the hole after thrashing through a dead wild rose bush and a tangle of blackberry vines that left his forearms peppered with drops of blood. He wasn't prepared for the order on the other side. The trim edges of the lawn, the precise lines as if Euclid himself had been pushing the mower. The two bistro tables, the chairs and chaises and cantilevered umbrella, all arranged in perfect balance. It was remarkable.

Looking back at his own yard—the dandelions blitzing across the lawn, the humps thrust up by ground squirrels, the pool nearly empty save for the opaque pond by the drain—he thought about something someone had said, that a man's mind is reflected in his surroundings. Meaning, of course, that a tidy home denotes a tidy mind. But it could be just as true, couldn't it, that a fully occupied mind has no time for the mundane chores of cleaning and scrubbing, for the idle worry of other people's opinions? An orderly world, it might be said, is the sure sign of an empty head.

And anyway, the dandelions added some color to the yard—the foot soldiers of summer, he liked to call them—and the squirrel burrows gave it character, a little contour to the unbroken flatness. As for the pool, there was a kind of sludgy comfort about it. At night the hose dripping into the deep end lulled him to sleep, and in the morning the sun glanced from its algaed surface with a soft, muted glow.

Back up on his patio, beneath the crooked shade of his sagging eaves, he watched a light breeze work through the razor-straight tops of the oleanders on the other side of the fence. He sipped his warm beer, in which he could taste a faint must from the pool. A blend of decay and renewal, muck and fish. He dozed, dodging troubling dreams that came hurtling toward him like pinballs. In the midst of them, he was yanked awake by the harsh scrape of metal across cement— a chair or a table wrenched across the neighbor's patio. He sat up, saw the back door snapped open. A man's head, round and slightly balding.

"Cin?" it called, sibilants whistling from between clamped teeth. "Cin!"

The girl—Cin, apparently—whose shadow Ludlow could see against the fence beneath the whorls of wisteria along the garage wall (the only unruly thing on the property), didn't answer. The head moved down the steps, crossed the patio and straightened whatever had been displaced. Ludlow thought he could hear breathing, slightly ragged, as if this little movement had required a disproportionate effort. After a minute the head climbed the steps again and went back inside, and the shadow in the corner slid slowly down the fence.

~

"It's short for Cindy, which you probably guessed."

"I thought maybe."

"I wish he wouldn't do that, shorten it like that. Cin. I mean, if that doesn't give you a complex."

"It's a pretty short name already."

"Exactly."

They were attaching a new hinge to the gate he'd forgotten was there, behind the wall of blackberry and pyracantha, until she'd wriggled through and popped her head out like a gopher. She could help, she'd said, looking around. Tidy things up, knock some of the brush back. Ludlow had reluctantly consented, and together they'd pulled the vines down and pried the gate free. He suspected it was the fish she was interested in.

"You're not a pedophile or anything are you?" she asked.

"No."

"Promise?"

"Cross my heart. I have a daughter myself."

"Where is she?"

"Oh, you know," he said, testing the swing of the gate.

"How would I know?"

"No, right." The pneumatic shock eased it back into place silently. "She's up north somewhere."

"Somewhere? I wish my dad was that laid back. I can't go down the street."

"Well, he cares about you."

"I'm sure you care about your daughter."

"Jeannie."

"Okay."

"Of course, yes. But it's how you measure these things that gets tricky. I mean, how you feel against what you do. Living up to your feelings."

"Are you like a psychologist or something?"

"No."

"You sound like one. My mom's one."

"You don't say."

"I do."

"Is she any good?"

"I wouldn't be surprised. She's been in bed a few months now though, so she's probably a little rusty." Behind them, the fish slurped a stray pellet from the surface. "Is that him?"

Ludlow didn't know whether the fish was male or female. He decided it probably didn't matter.

"That's him."

Cindy crouched and waddled slowly toward the edge of the pool, peered over the side into the murk.

"I wasn't sure what you were doing out here at first," she said. "Sitting on the diving board all the time."

"Now you know."

"Does he have a name?"

"No."

He had had one once, but Ludlow couldn't remember it.

Cindy grinned.

"How about A. Diem?"

"Very good."

"Get it?"

"I kind of saw that coming, to tell you the truth."

"No you didn't."

"I did."

"I don't believe you."

"All the same."

She pulled a loose strand of hair into her mouth and chewed it thoughtfully.

"Anyway, I'm not sure it's a carp," Ludlow said.

"Okay. How about Byron then?"

"Like the poet?"

"No, like the kid in my class. He looks like him. Around the mouth especially. And the eyes."

"Too bad for him."

"Tell me about it."

The surface of the pool rippled as a dorsal fin sliced through the algae. Byron flicked his tail, clearing a short-lived hole in the muck, then sank out of sight again.

～

"Are you coming to my graduation?"

"Of course."

Jeannie's voice had lost some of its childish warble, and her lisp was nearly gone.

"You'll need tickets. And my signature, of course."

"Okay."

"And can you talk to mother?"

"Is she there?"

"God no."

"Well, I haven't seen her—"

"You don't know where she is?"

"I have an idea."

A drawn-out sigh from Jeannie's end, the same sigh she'd used so effectively when petitioning for emancipation. Thirteen years old and outgrown her parents. But hasn't everybody by then?

"Well, if you do hear from her, tell her about graduation."

"I sure will, honey."

Jeannie laughed. "Honey," she said, and hung up.

The fish had been hers, three years old already when she'd left it behind as easily as she had them. Well past any goldfish lifespan Ludlow had anticipated. He wondered if it missed her, if it even remembered her. The man at the aquarium had said goldfish forgot everything they'd known after a single lap around the bowl. Everything fresh and new each time around. What a wonderful place! Look at that pirate's chest!

The man had also explained why the fish was no bigger after three years than it had been on its little stand at the fair when he'd won it for her, licking a dime on the sly to make it stick.

"They grow to the size of their containers."

A practical adaptation that didn't, unfortunately, apply to children. Jeannie had outgrown her container way ahead of time.

He turned the picture on the table toward him.

"This is better, isn't it honey?"

"I love you, Dad."

~

"I'd always thought I'd be a good father, before Jeannie was born. Even for a while after. It was quite a shock to hear I wasn't."

Cindy was lying on the diving board, her head hanging over the end.

"What did you do, hit her or something?"

"No!"

"I don't know. It must have been something bad."

"She had a list of our failings. Reasons she wasn't the person she thought she should be by then."

"Can I get her lawyer's name?"

Ludlow laughed. "You've got it all right over there. Give your folks a break."

She shrugged and tapped the canister of fish food, sprinkling a fine dust onto the water.

The sound he'd been hearing for a couple of weeks now started up again across the fence, and he saw Cindy flinch. He'd taken it at first for an animal—a raccoon caught in the barbed wire at the rail yard, or a cat eating a castoff fish hook—but he knew now that wasn't it. He wished it was.

"That's not much of a life, is it? Swimming in circles?"

"I don't know. What else is he going to do?"

"Learn to play the piano."

She let a little dribble of spit fall into the pool.

"Maybe we could clean it up some."

"You think he'd like that?"

Cindy thought about it.

"I could get in there with him. Swim around with him."

"I don't know."

"I'll do all the work."

"It's not that."

"What is it?"

Ludlow couldn't answer that one.

Byron went belly-up when they dropped him into the kiddie pool, one fin sticking up through the mat of algae they'd carried over with him.

Cindy danced from foot to foot, her breath whistling through her nose.

"What's going on?"

"I don't know."

"Well do something!"

That was the problem right there. You were always expected to do something, to know what needed to be done. But what if you didn't? What if you had no idea in the world what was called for?

He poked the fish with the handle of the rake, and Byron slowly righted himself. He flicked his tail and ducked under the algae.

"Just resting, I guess," Ludlow said.

Cindy turned away from him, sniffling. Ludlow looked at her back, the little hunched shoulders that weren't nearly up to what was being asked of them. Something was called for, he knew, another solution to another problem that was beyond him. He tapped the rake handle against his forehead. It never ended.

~

While Cindy worked the skimmer, scooping clots of algae and leaves from the pool, Ludlow sat in the shade and picked his guitar. Some time around lunch, her father came out into their yard and started up his string trimmer. They could hear him working his way around the perimeter of the patio, then along the fence line. Cindy stood with the skimmer resting on the pool bottom, following her father's movements with a barely perceptible pivot of her head. When he was done with the trimmer, he went after the stray blades with hand shears. Snip snip snip, regular as a bomb ticking.

Ludlow stumbled his way through "Folsom Prison Blues," muting the strings too heavily. Thuds like cardboard whacked with a spoon. He jumbled the words too, inserting bits of "Ring of Fire" and "Jackson" without knowing it.

In the middle of the last verse, Cindy's father stopped beside the gate. On this side, Cindy stopped cleaning and waited. Ludlow expected the gate to open and the man to step through. He'd want to know why his daughter kept disappearing through it, wouldn't he? There was a pull between them even he could feel. But neither of them said anything, and after a minute he moved on again.

Ludlow hit the last chord and listened to it die out in the clematis at the far corner of the yard. He frowned slightly. The same something stirred again down around his stomach, scratched against his duodenum like a cat wanting in.

"What did you think?" he called.

Cindy smiled and went back to cleaning.

Well now.

~

By the next day, there was just a brown pool of water in the deep end, all the solid matter had been scooped out by Cindy and deposited in a pile behind the broken bird feeder.

"You could use that for compost," she said.

"If I had a garden."

She looked at the sweet peas scrambling across a tangled nest of bamboo poles.

"Brown thumb," he said.

Somewhere underneath were a pair of tomato plants that Jeannie had planted years earlier, which continued to deliver a half-dozen misshapen tomatoes every summer without him lifting a finger—appropriately, she might have said. Such a diligent little girl. Kneeling in her little apron, carefully setting the plants in the hollows she'd dug out. Her rubber bumblebee boots clicking their heels behind her, while he did . . . what?

"We'd better knock off for today," he said.

Cindy dragged her arm across her forehead.

"We?"

"I've got to be somewhere."

"Tomorrow, then? We can fill it up?"

"Why not."

~

He did two quick songs, then walked hurriedly offstage and out of the coffee shop. He sounded like shit. His voice was raw and harsh, his fat fingers refused to stay where he put them. And all through it, and after, the crowd behaved the same as always. Cheers, whoops, pats on the back. "Nice set, Lud." "Classic, as usual." Big smiles and big laughs.

He had a few extra beers on the back patio. The night was warm and clear, and the moon, almost full, poured down on the yard, reaching into every bare patch on the lawn. A few mosquitoes circled over the pile of muck and around the kiddie pool. No lights blinking on and off like when he was a kid, fireflies floating over the grass. Jeannie had never seen a firefly, as far as he knew. He wondered if Cindy had. Probably not, not out here, on this far side of the mountains they'd somehow never managed to cross.

What did you chase after then? Mosquitoes and flies? Nothing to clap your hands around, to watch vanish and reappear in front of you. How are you supposed to live like that?

He looked at the pool, pictured it full—as it would be soon—of water like blown glass. Not a ripple on it, there was never any wind this time of year. The hose stuck in the shallow end gurgling, swiping back and forth like a water snake. He watched the water rise up to the lip of the tiles, past the line of caulk, saw the concrete darken as it washed over the cracked deck onto the edge of the lawn. It swelled like a bubble, up and up, pushing back the limbs of the pecan tree with him reflected in his chair, small and insignificant. A convex funhouse mirror of water in which he could see too the ratty house and yard, the smudged sky, time itself in all its folly and puniness.

He threw a bottle into the air—toward a point he guessed to be the apartment he lived in when he was twenty-six—watched it flash in the moonlight. He half expected it to bounce back, but of course it sailed right over the fence into Cindy's yard. His guitar's flight was shorter and even more disappointing, lumbering like an obese swan before it cracked against the pool deck and the D string popped loose. He swung it by the broken string in a wide arc, putting his back into it this time. The wind hummed across the sound hole. This was his kind of music. He'd been chasing the wrong thing all along.

Cindy found him the next morning lying at the base of the steps in the shallow end, curled between a broken lawn chair and a bleached-out Big Wheels. A drift of broken toys and tools and furniture was fanned around him as if they'd all washed up together on some foul tide. She climbed up on the diving board and waited there until he woke up, dangling her feet over what should have been a clear, rippling paradise of water.

"My mom's in the hospital."

"What?"

His mouth, when he swallowed, tasted like onions and blood.

"Or a hospice, whatever they call it. Are they the same thing?"

"Not quite."

"Because you don't come out, right?"

He tried to pull himself up into the lawn chair, but it was bent too far out of whack and threw him out again.

"They're just different."

Cindy nodded and pulled her towel around her shoulders. She was in her bathing suit, a pair of goggles clamped on her head.

"I thought maybe me and Byron could swim today."

Ludlow picked up the chair and a broken shovel and climbed with some difficulty over the debris and up the steps.

"The drain's still clogged."

"Oh."

"Maybe when you get back."

"I'm not going there."

"You should."

She shook her head.

"It'll be worse even than our house. Everything just so."

"They need it that way."

"I don't."

He brought out two cups of day-old coffee and handed one to her. How old were you supposed to be for coffee? He couldn't remember. She sniffed it and took a careful sip.

"Do you want sugar?"

"No thanks."

"I've got some Halloween candy if you're hungry."

"I thought you weren't a perv? Besides, it's nine in the morning. And June, so . . ."

"Just asking."

He sat on the back of the diving board and felt the pain slosh from one side of his head to the other, slamming against his temples.

"I'm not sure what happened here," he said.

Cindy kept her eyes down, studying the oily surface of the coffee.

"I mean, I know," he added, "but . . ."

"Whatever. It's your house."

"We can haul it out of there, it won't take that long."

"It doesn't matter."

"Sure it does."

Cindy stood up and tried to smile.

"I'm not mad or anything. Really."

Ludlow didn't believe her.

"C'est la vie, right?"

He nodded.

"Right?"

He nodded again, but he wasn't at all sure.

He didn't remember the cold hurting like this when he was a kid, water hurting. But nothing had, really; not for long anyway.

Byron floated aimlessly nearby, his fins paddling without much effect. Ludlow gave him a little push, and he drifted for a second before fanning his tail and darting back into the shadows by the steps.

"Where's your gumption, Byron?"

Ludlow did a slow lap, the water crisp and clear as he'd pictured it. It wouldn't stay this way long—chlorine, he figured, was out of the question—but for now it was okay. They could float like this, in their element, Ludlow and Byron. Effortlessly.

Later, after the shade had moved in, he dragged his mower and hand edger through the gate. It took him two passes to knock down the grass that had grown wild and unruly over the past couple of weeks. They'd get a good price, he was sure. It was an attractive, welcoming house. The kind of place you imagined happy families living.

Through the open gate, his own house looked shabbier than ever in comparison—except for the pool, gleaming bright as a new tooth in a wrecked smile.

He trimmed along the edge of the patio and down the fence line, then swept and hauled the clippings to the curb. It was a good job, professional, and he liked to think he would have done it even if they weren't paying him.

When he'd finished, it was almost three o'clock. Jeannie would be walking into the auditorium about now. Maybe looking around for her mother and father, maybe knowing better. If things were as they should be, he would have been sitting in the audience with his wife, beaming as people were said to do. He took his shoes off and stepped onto the diving board. Jeannie had done well enough on her own these past years, he was sure she'd be fine without him. And if not . . .

Byron hung close to the wall in the shallow end, slipping along the tiles, hesitant to come out into open water. You couldn't blame him, really. He hadn't asked for this. The sun must have seemed impossibly bright, and the transparent world rippling out around him strange and new and unnatural.

The board strained under Ludlow, the anchor bolts clicking as he sprang up and hung in the air for a moment. At the top, he could see over the fence into the empty yard, into the rooms with their curtains gone. The view came and went as he bounced—the not quite spotless patio, the scuff marks where the furniture had been, the wisteria working its way up the roof of the garage. Here and gone, here and gone. A familiar enough phenomenon.

THE ARMCHAIR GARDENER

ED KOLSTONE SAT BACK IN his big, comfortable chair—one eye on *Cuthbertson's Gardening Almanac* and the other on the leaves beginning to die so colorfully outside his window—and recited once more, like a mantra, the first line of his obituary:

Ed Kolstone was a man of his word: When he predicted rain, it never failed to materialize.

He tallied the attendees, a childish exercise. Who would come to pay their respects after such a long silence? The list was short, as any such list should be, quality of affection rather than quantity being the yardstick. Someone in the back wept, a woman whose face was obscured behind her chiaroscuroing veil. Her wailing rose louder and louder until it drowned out even the leaf blower next door. Pigeons rose from the architrave.

Far down in the knuckle of his big toe a throbbing

began working its way up. He followed its progress, as though it were an ant or some other insect hauling itself uphill. It itched, but he'd be damned if he was going to scratch it. He had willpower, had always had at least that.

He gritted his teeth, felt the vein pulsing in his temple.

The bug moved up inexorably.

What more could you expect of an insect? People in general expected too much of too many things. It was a mistake he'd never made. When the local AAA team, *The Beekeepers*—for example—lost 6-5 in the playoffs, he didn't explode the way so many of his neighbors did.

"What the fuck? Bunting on two strikes?"

"There's always next year," he'd said. Well, there was and there wasn't.

When his wife left him, he took that in stride too. Looking down at him in his chair, this same chair.

"If you got up off your ass once in a while."

"True enough, I should."

"I need more than this. There's got to be more."

"I'm sure there is. I hope you find it."

She didn't bother closing the door after her, and it was a good eight hours before Ed got up to do it. When he did, he saw a dog he didn't recognize with its head stuck in the chain link. It was a small dog, with an even smaller head. It tried to bark at him, but could only manage a kind of squeak. Two days later it was gone, he wasn't sure how. Possibly it had lost enough weight—the head, too, contains appreciable amounts of fat—to wriggle out.

He looked down at his pendant legs, remembered how his father had referred to his feet as dogs: "My dogs are barking today." Kicking off his shoes and propping his feet on the coffee table. He too had died young.

Was Ed Kolstone young? He'd always thought of himself that way, but now, at fifty-two, it might not be true anymore. He hiked up his pant leg, stared at the pale skin of his calf. He couldn't see the clot, but it was there. Spreading like a pudding beneath the tissue.

Gather together the detritus of your life and deposit it carefully, layering gently and loosely, in the compost bin of your memory.

He read the almanac entry twice.

"As you wish, Cuthbertson," he said to himself.

Though, clearly, Cuthbertson was losing it.

⌒

He ran and ran, the tall weeds grabbing at him, burrs latching onto his pants. He ran until his lungs were raw, up the steep incline of the levee and down the other side.

Onto the horse trail peppered with road apples.

A beaver slapped the water off to his side and dove.

He was fast, he knew it, but not quite fast enough. The coach cut him. He could stay on in Equipment, but who wanted that?

He'd always been told that with enough drive you could do anything you set your mind to, and it was a decided disappointment to find out that wasn't true. There were faster people, smarter people. He was somewhere down in the fat middle of the curve in every area that mattered.

He ground up to the top of the rise below the rapids and there she was—he would always remember it like that, a revelation. Donna Harris, her long hair trailing down her bare back, a silhouette out of an illuminated manuscript. Her breasts pointing toward shore where her clothes had been carelessly dropped. She turned her head slowly; her hair swept back and forth like the hanging strips in a car wash.

Jesus, was that the best he could do?

He watched just long enough to permanently implant the image, then turned around and ran back the way he'd come.

That bend in the river became for him like Lourdes. The light fell differently on that stretch of trail, the holy water sparkling beneficently below.

Ever afterward he could call her back at will, though never before quite like this—just outside his living room window, pounding a For Sale sign into the lawn across the street.

~

"So the Mitchells are leaving?" he said.

"Yes. Moving on."

She brushed her hair out of her face—the same hair—as she turned and smiled at him.

He smiled back. Waited.

"We went to school together," he said.

"Sure."

"Ed Kolstone."

"Yes, I remember."

Her toe tapped just perceptibly on the walkway.

"Are you still running?" she asked.

"Wow. You do remember."

"I said I did. I saw you sometimes."

"Huh."

He was favoring his good leg, leaning a little to port. She glanced down, then politely away.

"I've pretty much hung up the shoes," he said. "Getting older, you know?"

"Aren't we all."

"Probably."

Behind him, jumbled voices, the presence of bodies.

"Hi!" Donna called over his shoulder.

He moved out of the way to let a tightly packed family pass: The father thin with a very thick mustache, the mother and oldest daughter smiling under hijabs.

"We love it," the father said.

"Wait till you see the inside."

They jostled one another to be the first through the door that then closed behind them.

Behind his own door, Ed looked down disapprovingly at the sunken seat of the chair. The leather had cracked and turned darker than the rest. It was unseemly.

He brought some old leg weights in from the garage and strapped them on while he watched *Jeopardy* and *Antiques Roadshow*. The insect scuttling deep in his leg tickled.

~

After an initial, understandable period of wariness, the Pourans settled in. They waved to him on the way to their car, or walking down the opposite sidewalk toward the park. They could see him through the front window. On his throne, as Soraya called it.

He heard the car speed off on a Tuesday night, but didn't see who had thrown the eggs at their house.

"Don't judge us all by that," he said.

Their smiles weren't quite as bright, but they were still there.

After a lawn job, a broken window, and two more egg-throwing incidents, the smiles went into full retreat.

He tried to reassure them, to tell them those people were not emblematic, but he wasn't entirely convinced himself. He hardly knew his neighbors. They had always looked at him, too, with suspicion—hurrying past his house with their kids or dogs, shaking their heads faintly behind tinted SUV windows. Squinting through fireworks smoke at the block party he wasn't invited to.

"This is America," he said.

By way of reassurance.

～

Donna waved to him from her car across the street.

"Isn't it awful?" she said.

"Yes."

"Some people," she said, shrugging.

"Some people what?"

Summer had returned overnight. Indian Summer, as they once called it, he didn't know why. Sweat glistened on her skin—as he remembered it, as it had always been. The air along the recollected river cooled him, leaning against his fence.

"They don't like change," she said.

He nodded. That was probably true.

"I love it myself."

And he meant it, which surprised him.

"Well, you're a rare one."

She turned the BMW's A/C on full, he could hear the fan whirring cleanly. It blew her hair around her face as though she were standing at the edge of a canyon, wind rising from the depths to stir the hearts of those above.

182

She left a puddle of condensation behind on the pavement. If he tilted his head just right and didn't stick too strictly to reality, it was shaped like a heart.

~

The floorboards creaked under the armchair. He changed position again, but couldn't get comfortable. In his dreams now, he was running again. He'd wake up drenched in sweat, the sheets coiled tightly around him. In one dream, the track coach was making love to Donna Harris behind the backstop. He could see the coach's fat jiggling, Donna's breasts lifting and falling. When she threw her head back and screamed, Ed did the same.

The Pourans came and went silently now, never loitering for long in the open. They looked at him through the peephole when he knocked, but wouldn't open the door.

"I'm sorry," he said.

The peephole cover slid back into place with a squeak.

He imagined them sitting inside silently, each in his or her own armchair.

~

He'd ruined the homecoming float, several people claimed, even though he'd only stepped on a corner, smashed a handful of paper flowers. He was half drunk, unable to commit fully even to that. He staggered more than necessary, playing it up.

MARCHING TO OUR FUTURES was spelled out in yellow and green, with the S a little splayed where he'd trod on it. It struck him as excessively militaristic for a dance.

Someone pushed him toward the open garage door. He tripped on a bucket of paint and took out half of the TO.

"Get out!" Donna screamed. Looming. Her eyes disdainful, a little spit in the corner of her perfect mouth.

"You're beautiful."

"Do something," she said to someone behind him.

He was hoisted and heaved into the side yard beside the recycling bin. By his face was a stepping stone little Donna had inscribed years ago with a handprint and a smiley face.

"Asshole," he thought he heard. But that couldn't be. He kissed the childish scrawl.

~

He hurriedly undid the ankle weights when he heard the car slow, followed by the thud and splat of eggs. He had to drive with one weight still attached as he chased them through the once-cherished streets of his neighborhood—ratty now around the edges, and possibly inside—into a new development with a counterfeit English name: Wolton Hills, never mind the lack of anything resembling a hill. The houses were tall and narrow, each trimmed and corniced in a bastardy of styles. The yards were neatly maintained with not a single visible garden.

The car pulled into one of the wide driveways, and two teenagers got out. Whooping and high-fiving. By the open front door, Donna Harris clapped and laughed. Ed noticed her smile wasn't quite as fresh as it had been once, and saw the silk of her hair in the harsh blaze of security lights take on a metallic gleam like broken piano strings. She ushered the boys inside—for cookies and milk, maybe. A lecture on purity and maximizing commissions.

~

The little dog—he'd reappeared not long after the Pourans moved in—barked at Donna as she tried to hug Mrs. Pouran and Soraya. Their arms hung limp at their sides.

Donna kicked at the dog without breaking the embrace. The dog didn't budge.

After she'd driven off, Ed fed the dog a can of cat food he had lying around.

"Good dog."

He waved to the Pourans as they piled into the U-Haul, glancing sideways at the For Sale sign Donna had replanted in the lawn, but they ignored him. He couldn't blame them. Was there any telling us apart?

That night in his dream, clumps of Donna's hair streamed past him, uprooted like grass in a hurricane.

She called to him the next morning from the Pourans' open front door.

"Airing it out!"

In what he hoped was a calm fashion, he pulled the For Sale sign out of the lawn and threw it into the street. Donna looked at him the way an oncology nurse might look at a flagging patient.

"I knew you were there," she said. "At the river. Watching me."

"It wasn't planned."

"I didn't mind."

"No, I guess not."

She shrugged.

"It's what I had."

Ed heard a faint whistling sound, time slipping its gears on the grade.

"Me too," he said.

Donna laughed, snorted once.

"Not quite," she said. Then she turned smartly on her clean white sneakers and strode off into the dusk of the emptied house.

⌢

He hadn't run in so long. He could feel the blood beginning to move, loosening up like cold syrup. He jogged past the little gate Bita Pouran had briefly swung from, pushing with one foot to set it going. The little dog barking, nipping at her feet. They had thought it belonged to him.

He cut through the park to the levee, over it and down to the stretch of river he'd run along way back when. The water was down, the bank littered with trash. Plastic bags hung in the trees like decorations from the last high water. As he wound along the trail, he resumed composing his obituary.

A man before and behind his time. A dedicated gardener bereft of his garden.

Somewhere around the bike bridge he moved on to the elegy. The church was nearly flooded with tears by the time he hit the horse trail. The smell was familiar: horse shit and dust, something dead off in the blackberries.

The river widened and turned shallow where Donna had appeared to him. A loose band of geese that hadn't bothered to migrate back north floated lazily near shore. Cuthbertson's Almanac in his back pocket, Ed shook off the bug moving inexorably up his vein.

Plant early, for the long season will undo all but the most resilient of seedlings.

Though Cuthbertson had died twenty years earlier, in a light plane crash over the desert, his almanac continued to be issued, with some revisions, year after year. Ed had relied on it in mapping out his own years. He wouldn't abandon it now, of course, but he would pay a little closer attention. It was astonishing to him, for instance, that he could still mistake a weed for a flower.

He put his funeral on hold as he turned off the trail and plunged headlong into a stand of alders hung thick with wild grape.

HIDDENFOLK

THE VIEW IN EVERY DIRECTION was the same—sloping tables of wind-scraped land tilted this way and that as if they'd been dropped by a running child. There were no trees, just an incongruous carpet of bright green grass sown across volcanic rock. Low clouds scudded past overhead, the sky bearing down on Pete Harmon so that he seemed to be on the summit of a high peak rather than twenty feet above sea level. That's how he would describe Iceland to Tower—a mountain breaking through the ocean.

So then, he was lost at sea.

He laughed and patted himself figuratively on the back for being able to laugh in such a situation, lost in a harsh country of ice and rock. He wished Tower were here to see it; it might have changed his opinion.

He didn't try to tell himself it was fine out here on his

own, that he didn't miss Tower's company. Their trips were a tradition, one of the few he had left, a yearly reprieve from the pressures of his practice. He was happiest during the months of preparations—poring over maps, researching patterns, caravanning down to the fly shop— and on the flight over, before they touched down. Watching the threads of water flash under the wing, the liquid shimmer of possibility. It wasn't the same without him, and Pete knew this solo trip would be his first and last.

The core of the earth was close under his feet, contained by a thin skin of rock and gravelly soil. He bent beside a geothermal vent to let the steam warm him, though he suspected it probably chilled him even more in the long run. He heard rumblings in the distance, hungry belly growls like thunder rolling. This was newborn country, geologically speaking. He stomped his feet, clapped his hands against his sides. His lips were too cold to whistle properly, but he tried anyway. Squeaked out a pitiful, thin peep, and laughed again.

You could summon the hiddenfolk, Einar had told him, with a whistle.

"They run this place," he'd explained, while they detoured a half-hour around a boulder in the road he claimed the hiddenfolk had put there. "Not the government, not the Prime Minister, not Bjork." He snorted and bounced over a lip of calcified mud at the edge of the road. "She might be hiddenfolk, though, now I think about it. One of their bastards."

They could change the landscape itself, Einar alleged, move mountains and rivers, even alter the sky. Their powers were vague and enormous, and they used them according to a code only they understood. Out of simple mischief sometimes, but at other times directed toward more serious ends—to protect the helpless, and to punish the deserving.

"'Little gods brought to life,'" Einar said, spitting a dollop of snuss into a coffee cup. "Halldor Laxness said that. He was a smart man and a great writer, but a little too clever for Iceland."

Pete squinted out into the empty landscape. How nice it would be to believe in such things, fairytale creatures behind every stroke of good and bad luck. At the core of every disease, nestled down in each corrupt cell. He could just whistle over Cicely, promise a favor in return for a favor.

He saw her thin and frail in her tidy room, the disease moving invisibly beneath her skin like termites burrowing, and saw Tower at the window looking out on the field behind the hospital, the muddy pool of rainwater. He thought out there was where life was lived, that the two worlds—inside/outside, sickness/health—were mutually exclusive. But Pete knew they existed on a single plane of possibility, that the wall between them was as soft and permeable as a cloud bank.

He stepped out into the hall and breathed in the vaguely ammoniac air, listened to the hospital's soothing metronomic heart, and felt a contentment he felt nowhere else but on a river. It was a world that he understood, and admired. Sometimes as he made his rounds or took the long way down to the OR, he would stop in the middle of a hallway and listen to the whir of the ducts like water flowing, low voices rippling. He'd watch the carpet turn liquid, the silver backs of trout flick through doorways.

He crooked his finger under the cork of the rod handle, felt it balance perfectly. It was a beautiful creation, supple, hand-wrapped bamboo. It had been a gift from his father before their first big trip to the Yellowstone, passed on to him in an oddly ceremonious moment—his dad's head down, offering it butt-first like a sword, eyes smooth and glassy as a junkie's. It was an attempt at connection, Pete understood, however tardy. He decided he'd give it to Cicely when he got back.

The rod tip sawed between two clusters of stars showing through the half-twilight. Maybe he could dowse his way back to the car, let the rod point the way. He turned in a slow arc, panning across the sky where the unfamiliar stars jumbled together like spilled salt. Jesus Christ, he muttered, what stupid fucking— just before the rod picked out the low-slung cabin tucked into a cleft in the rock.

There was no lock on the thick slab of a door, which swung open surprisingly easily. A cast iron stove sat in the corner, hunched on bowed iron legs, its paunch stuffed already with wood. He got it going with one match and flopped down on the floor like a dog worn out from chasing its tail. Cicely returned as he descended into a sleep like a fall, as she often did, without ceremony or demands. Accompanied by the song he played when he was in the OR—"Lost Cause"—and that he'd found himself unknowingly singing at her bedside. He'd thought at one time there was something funny about it in the context of the OR, but he'd almost buckled with shame when Cicely looked up at him from the bed with that little crease across her forehead, and Tower clenched his hands into fists at the window.

He woke to words he couldn't understand, grunts and trills like animal sounds. There wasn't much light in the room, but in the face hanging over him he could clearly discern the distinctive features of Down syndrome.

"I couldn't find my car," he said.

The girl said more that he couldn't understand, then opened his creel where two fat char sat on a bed of grass. She lifted them and turned their heads so that they faced her. She said something to them softly before gutting them on the counter.

They ate both the fish, along with some shriveled potatoes fried in butter. The girl laid the fish bones carefully and neatly on her plate as she ate, studying their pattern and every now and then tsking or nodding. She turned the plate expectantly to Pete at one point, to show him some divined meaning, but he saw only a scatter of bones tied loosely by strips of skin.

After they'd eaten, she lifted his rod and pack and held them out.

"Nordura," she said.

Pete recognized the name, one of the rivers on his list.

"Lead the way," he said.

She smiled her wide smile again, her face as smooth as the flank of their breakfast char.

They followed a long incline up out of the valley, along the spine of a glacial moraine that could have been set down a week ago. The girl reached the crest well before him, and immediately began jumping up and down and pointing at something. At the river, Pete thought, until he reached the top and saw billows of smoke curling from a wide mountain in the distance. Drifting toward them in a flat-bottomed plume.

"Eyjafjöll! Eyjafjöll!" she cried.

The smoke puffed and swirled like a time-lapse film, black cauliflower blooms spilling upward from the volcano, then curling back on themselves. Swollen lobes merging like cells, splitting and mutating.

———

Pete sometimes imagined that Cicely was his own daughter—he saw them watching movies together, playing Scrabble, cooking not very good meals and laughing at the results. And he saw them at other times too, when he could hear himself scolding.

It was probably too late for him to have kids of his own. Fifty next year. He'd have to marry a girl the same age as most of his friends' kids. Cicely's age. It was too lecherous to contemplate.

He tried not to think about what he was missing, the closeness that he saw between Cicely and Tower, their tangled nerves and hearts. He sidestepped the question of posterity, who'd be left after him to remember, to carry on. Because what was there to carry on, really? He was an easily replaced face on a medical group's website, a cog in a machine. Traveling? Fishing? Did that qualify as a legacy? It was something, anyway, something you could turn to when you turned away from other things.

They reached the river to find black ash flakes falling on the water and dissolving in bursts. The girl stuck her tongue out to catch one of the flakes, spat and tried to scrape the taste away.

He rigged up his rod, hoping the reel wouldn't foul.

The falling ash flicked past like scratches on an old film. He thought about collecting some to take back, to show Tower, maybe give some to Cicely. To provide evidence of the world still being born. To demonstrate that, despite recent reports, they weren't at the end of everything.

He cast a wooly bugger out to the eddy line, closed his eyes and pictured the contours of the river beneath the surface. Watching the fly drift through, anticipating the hit. It was a habit he'd developed when he was a kid, fishing along murky ditches and dry fields. He would watch the hook floating, feel the water washing over him in a continuous, unbreakable sheet. Later, when he moved on to sleeker, cleaner rivers, he would see the refracted images of peaks and rimrock, the speckled stones at the waterline. It was all so beautiful, and it left him with a craving—the only frustrating part—wanting badly to somehow take it in, to taste it, to make it a part of him.

He still remembered the feeling just before Tower pulled him out of the Blackfoot that time, the moment he gave in and stopped fighting. His arms and legs unburdening, his chest relaxing, everything sharp and clear as he stood on the border looking across. It terrified him still when he thought about how willing he'd been to give in, the resentment like bile when he was yanked back.

It had passed quickly, of course, with his first gulped breath (though it returned unexpectedly from time to time, tugging at his sleeve). A chest-burning rush of love shot through him, and he promised right there—tearfully, ridiculously—to be the watchdog of Tower's newborn daughter. To let nothing happen to little Cicely. Knowing that she would not always be little Cicely, and still believing himself capable of keeping such a promise.

She cried at her baptism, the icy water splashing across her forehead, running into her eyes. They were tied immediately in that way, bonded by water. Later, he and Tower together taught her to fish the little creek near their house. Pete would come up for the weekend, and they would hike out together through the woods to the chalk creek. She was more interested in the birds nesting in the low cliffs and the viceroy butterflies hovering over the creekside asters, but it didn't matter. Fishing was to a large extent an excuse, Pete had known that for some time.

When she was first admitted to Mercy, he tried to replicate the connection by way of a pet betta. It was very much against the rules, but he knew no one would call him on it. No nurse or PA certainly. The bowl sat on the sill in the little window alcove, the fish swimming aimlessly inside and periodically throwing itself against the glass. You could hear it, a little ping every so often. Then it would float slowly toward the surface before recovering and swimming back into its corner behind the little spray of coral.

Tower took it away before it died, something Pete himself should have done. Its color had faded quickly, no longer iridescent blue but a blotchy gray like the belly of a lamprey. It recovered more and more slowly each time it charged the glass, floating for longer periods on the surface, gills working.

"You're an idiot sometimes," Tower said.

A nun passed them in the hall, her head lowered to hide her smile. They were always shuffling past, fingering their beads, their black shoes clicking on the tiles.

"I thought it would cheer her up."

"Just fix her. That'll cheer her up."

"I can't."

"Yeah you can."

He watched the nun's back, the black cloth off which everything flowed like water. They made him uneasy, the nuns. He couldn't help feeling they were working against him, with their magic book and their incantations. He'd hear them whispering with patients, catch them glancing secretively at him. In their eyes, he was a partner to the disease.

"I want to bring in a specialist," he said.

"Nobody else," Tower said.

"It's the rule for this kind of thing, Matt. You don't take care of your own."

"Bullshit. That's the opposite of the rule."

"Not here. Not in medicine. You don't treat family, that's the rule."

"We're not family."

"Close enough." He thought that might strike Tower as touching, but it didn't. "Your judgment goes when you're too close. You can't make the hard choices."

It was true, whether or not it was the real reason for his decision. He considered calling down the hall to the nun, having her explain to Tower how weak and faulty people are, how they can't be depended on to carry the day.

"It's like a fishing guide," he said. "Think of him like that."

"Jesus."

"No, really. He knows where to look. And where not to waste his time."

When Pete brought Kinnell in, all the way from

Pittsburgh, Tower wouldn't even shake his hand. Kinnell stood there with his hand out, his thin, bluish wrist covered with a fine dusting of talc, the long fingers twitching like worms.

"This guy's the best," Pete said to Cicely. "The best in the world."

Cicely tried to smile, to ignore her father's turned back and be the good patient, but she knew just as well as Tower what it was all about. She had never named the betta. She wasn't a kid anymore, she knew how these things went.

~

The river smelled of sulfur, a plume of steam rose from the far bank. The fish had adapted to it, Pete supposed, taking in the gas and converting it to belly colors and parr marks. Beauty transformed from poison. That was life, right? Though just as often it flowed the other way.

The girl was looking at her reflection in the water, speckled with falling ash. Her broken stream of talk was a whisper now, but whether it was directed at him or the fish Pete couldn't tell.

He took out the pocket dictionary he'd picked up before he left, but the words in it were so foreign, so crammed with peculiar letter combinations that he couldn't tell one from another. He tried to form a sentence from the bits Einar had taught him at the lodge, but she just smiled back, a bright, tolerant smile that was beginning to wear on him.

There was a peculiar warmth under the cover of the ash, close and dry. The ground was covered with it like black snow, and a layer had formed on the rock that was slick as ice underfoot. This would be a story to tell—volcano fishing. He opened his pack and rooted around for his camera.

Cicely kept an album of all of his and Tower's trips, the pictures her way of joining them, of being part of the long chain of friendship. One picture—a shot of him and Tower on the Firehole River, their arms on each other's shoulders—she'd had made into a sweatshirt. She wore it the day she went into the hospital. Pete found it hanging in the closet, empty and limp-armed, when he went to get a new bedpan liner.

He and Tower had discussed bringing her along on a trip soon, maybe next year to the Ponoi River. She was old enough, she could handle it no problem. Pete himself had taught her to cast and she'd learned quickly—roll casts, double hauls—she wouldn't have any trouble keeping up. He had even suggested bringing her this year, but Tower had nixed it. Then she fell down at school, out cold, her belly distended and a fever burning through her. Pete wished he'd insisted on the invitation, if only to let her know she was welcome. You wait too long sometimes, and the chance goes away for good.

He took a picture looking down the river, and another across at the mountain smoking in the distance. If only he could record it all—the sharp gunpowder smell, the sound that was almost like an inversion, the river and the sizzling flakes receding toward some central mass. The sensation of being perfectly still inside a shifting pocket of sky and earth.

A school of char swam past below him, moving erratically, darting and weaving like bacteria under a scope. They veered from the wall below him out again into the current. A little downstream, the girl saw them too. She ran to the edge of the ledge calling, sliding at the last second on the slick of ash.

Pete heard the crack of bone ahead of the splash, saw her flop into the water and sink. He waited for her to claw to the surface and suck in a breath, but there was no struggle, no thrashing of arms and legs, just the water closing over and weaving on through the rocks. The distorted image of the girl hung just beneath the surface, her short hair like a halo of rusty river grass. The current pushing her into the rocks, bouncing her against them.

~

We live in water until we're born, and resemble fish quite closely in the womb. Pete considered the vestigial tail and gill slits, saw a time lapse of the developing fetal face, the halves coming together, seams joining, the nose moving down from the forehead into place. So many things, he knew, could go wrong along the way.

He followed the bank as far as he could, the girl bobbing up then disappearing, until the river bent into a canyon and there was nowhere to walk anymore. He looped around, over a scarp and down the other side to where the river opened back out, but he couldn't find her again. Looking up into the canyon, he could see staggered steps of rapids and pools, any number of places where she could have been caught. He let himself believe for a minute that she'd clambered out somewhere, but he knew she hadn't. She was up there somewhere, nestled in a gravel bed or wedged in the crook of a boulder. Reversing the process that had created her—her lungs turning back into gills, her arms and legs fanning into fins again.

Trying to find his way back to the cabin, Pete mistook a knobbed volcanic outcrop for a different one they'd passed that morning and turned west instead of north. Lost again, he topped a rise and found himself on the shoulder of the road he'd driven down the day before, his car cloaked in ash a hundred yards off.

The engine turned, miraculously, the radio booming to life. Icelandic voices laughed, jabbered. Someone started singing, maybe Bjork, a wail that made him clamp his teeth. He looked in the rearview mirror—lines of ash around his red eyes, along the rim of his jaw. His skin smeared gray in a cracked mask.

Look what you've done to me.

～

"Devil fuck," Einar said. "You're alive."

"Am I?"

He laughed and slapped Pete on the back.

"Americans," he said. "Crazy all the time."

A group of Germans had arrived while he was gone. They nodded grimly.

Einar fixed him a plate of sheep's head and set two beers by his plate.

"Where did you go? We looked all day for you."

"I'm not sure. I ended up at the Nordura."

"You took a wrong turn then."

The split sheep's head stared past him, teeth gritted and lipless.

"Were there fish?" one of the Germans asked.

"There's always fish," Einar said. "Even when you're lost."

Pete tried to smile, thinking of the rivers as he'd seen

them when he first arrived. The clear water, the pristine banks. Now he saw ash sputtering on the surface and frantic schools of char spinning downstream.

"The Nordura's a good river," Einar said. "You got lucky. Good luck with the bad luck."

Pete popped an eye out of the sheep's head and pushed it to the side of his plate. The Germans sipped their beer and took pictures out the window of the low sun behind the ash cloud. Picture after picture.

"There's a girl lives out that way," Einar said. "Her name's Blin. It means 'she stares.' She's different, I don't know what you call it in English. We call it Downs-heiken-ni. A big round face. Happy."

"Down syndrome."

"She has names for all the fish in the Nordura. She says she can tell them apart."

"Is that right?"

"It's a nice cabin she has too. Strong and warm."

Pete pulled cautiously at the sheep's tongue.

"Wait," Einar said, reaching across the table. He lifted the tongue and smacked the hyoid bone with the back of his knife. "If you don't do this, a child will never grow to speak."

One of the Germans laughed.

"You have too many superstitions."

"Try living here without them."

~

While he was in the big room with Einar and the Germans, the lies came easily to him. He even started to believe them, to grow comfortable around them. What could anyone have done at that point? She was gone, anything he said would have just brought up more questions. Later, alone in his room at the back of the lodge, the lies became harder to accommodate. He told himself various things: If he'd gone in after her, for instance, chances are he wouldn't have come out again. The water was cold and swift, and he wasn't much of a swimmer. What good was a sacrifice like that?

"What is a physician's most important trait?" his first-year clinical instructor had asked them. They had all answered predictably—compassion, technical expertise, preparedness. And the professor, Hendricksen, had shaken his head, run his tongue across his upper lip at each wrong answer.

"It's being willing to walk away," he'd finally said. Smug and proud in his spotless lab coat. Pete had ridiculed the answer ever since, had modeled his practice around proving Hendricksen wrong. And now here he was.

Perhaps everyone is a coward, he thought, the only difference is they're never tested to the point of discovery. The moment of truth never arrives. And within that beautiful bubble, it's a simple matter to believe you're who you want to be.

He watched the night go slightly darker, and closed his eyes. A low buzz of electricity moved through his mind as he lay there. Someone watching would have seen his face twitch, his eyes jerking behind their lids as the vague feeling of something forgotten grew stronger, a thunderstorm moving across dry fields. Then it was there, on top of him, arcing through him.

The rod. Cicely's rod.

He pulled his boots on. The Germans and Einar had

all gone to bed. The downstairs room was empty, the last of the fire crackling its thousand red eyes. Outside it was still twilight, as it always seemed to be. He drove for the first few miles with the lights off, watching the landscape materialize and disappear as he moved through it. He found the road after one wrong turn, and pulled over where his old tracks were still visible in the gravel.

The water seemed less violent when he looked down on it from the ledge, the current almost sluggish. A body would linger for some time before drifting out, you would think. But you couldn't count on things like currents. Or rivers in general. A river was never the same river twice, as somebody had said. Giving them names was an act of plain desperation, a hopeless effort to hold them in state.

He found the rod where he'd left it, propped in a notch between two rocks. The bamboo, yellow and translucent as old bone, almost glowed. He lifted it, waggled the tip. It was soft and responsive, an extension of him.

"It's not as hard as everybody thinks," Cicely said as he dozed in the visitor's chair. She'd been asleep when he came in after his rounds. The medication rose and ebbed in her like that, bringing her suddenly awake and just as suddenly dragging her back down into sleep.

"What's not?"

"Living with this thing. Whatever it is."

"Isn't it?"

"Not really. It's part of me now, you know?"

There was a name for what she was beginning to feel, though he couldn't remember what it was. A Stockholm syndrome sort of effect, an irrational attachment to the thing that was killing you.

"It's hard for other people," he said.

"I know it is, that's the worst. But I wish you'd tell them it's okay. Really."

"I don't think I can."

Her eyes fluttered. The drugs were taking her again.

"At least tell yourself. You can do that much," she said.

But he couldn't. Not so he'd believe it.

~

He could hear the mountain's periodic rumble flowing in and out of the hiss of wind that had come up and whisked now through the tufts of tundra grass and through the bored holes in the rock. A shrill, warbling whistle that moved with him as he made his way up the slope.

He wanted a last look at the mountain, at the bulk of it on the horizon with the birth of the world underway. The ash cloud was breaking up. Out over the valley only scattered bits were left, pixely tufts dissipating like static over the little clusters of hiddenfolk moving toward him. He knew what they were without being told, as if he'd always lived among them. Their eyes blinked through the haze, their pale, streaked skin—which normally blended with the landscape—nearly translucent against the backdrop of the ash cloud. They moved quickly, and it wasn't long before they surrounded him in numbers, pushing and jeering.

He thought he saw Blin in the throng, standing a head taller and smiling her guileless smile as they herded him toward the cliff edge. The water here, he knew, would be colder than the Blackfoot, colder even than the Clark Fork. Near ice, a degree or two above freezing. How long would he last? Minutes probably.

They sang and chanted: We are here, we are here, all of us are here. He could smell their breath, close to the smell of the ash plume—smoke and the aftermath of fire, melting earth. One jumped on his shoulder, bit his ear. He felt blood start down his jaw. A blade sliced across his Achilles tendon. He lurched forward, half walking and half falling.

~

"So you're going," Tower said. "In the middle of this."

"There's nothing more I can do."

He was picturing the unreal landscape of Iceland, savoring its remoteness and strangeness. He could lose himself there, he thought. Anyway, he already had his ticket and had paid the guide. "It's just a week."

"Right."

"I'll be in touch. I'll check in with the staff."

"Sure," Tower said. "Life goes on." He was looking past Pete, out the window toward the hospital chapel and the rehab center. He looked older, but then they were all subject to that.

Cicely smiled, as she always did, her smile free of everything but love.

"Bring back some fat pictures," she said. Their joke.

Out in the hallway, a nun shuffled past, gave a little bow.

"Where is he?" Pete demanded. "That asshole god of yours?" To get a reaction, he guessed, to shake up the smug black-and-white stoicism and crack the beatific smile. He wanted to tear her habit off and make her face things naked like the rest of them.

"He works with love, doctor. Whatever you may say."

He passed a room where Rick Dobson was talking to a patient in the calm, smooth tones of a hypnotist. Impeccable bedside manner; a blessing, the nuns all said. If only Pete could do that, go back to Cicely's room, pull the chair close to her bed and talk to her like that. Tell her everything he knew, not just about fishing and rivers, but everything. The truth. How hard could it be?

The air circulating through the ward was cold and sterile. It would be like that in Iceland, everything scrubbed clean by wind. Nothing hidden, no traps or surprises, because there was nowhere to hide. He could see it: a beautiful emptiness going on and on. Just a few sheep here and there, and every so often a river.

ACKNOWLEDGEMENTS

The stories that make up *The Middle Ground* took their sweet time arriving, and might easily have been left by the roadside if it wasn't for the patience and encouragement of my wife Diane and my daughter Romy. Their steady love and ruthless confidence eased me forward against considerable currents, and it's for them I wanted to make something strange and—if not beautiful, at least companionable—an odd artifact they might be proud of.

My mother and father, for mysterious reasons, chose to love me unreservedly, and I can't thank them enough for that. My brother and sisters formed a net we alternately held out under one another, only occasionally flinching.

It's safe to say this book wouldn't exist without the belief, kindness, and tireless work of Philip Elliott. He took a chance on the evidence of two stories, and dove in headfirst. Into the Void, which he founded and raised quickly to prominence, has been a welcoming home to me. I have nothing but admiration and gratitude for his solid judgment and advice, and his chutzpah in tackling this adventure.

And then there are the friends who did what friends do. Yeah, I'm looking at you.

My thanks to the following publications in which some of these stories first appeared:

Eleven Eleven, "Tule Fog"; *Crazyhorse*, "Silo"; *Into the Void*, "Ice Flowers" and "Coast Starlight"; *Elm Leaves Journal*, "Double Helix"; *Atticus Review*, "Lake Mary Jane"; *Laurel Review*, "Crossing to Lopez"; *SmokeLong Quarterly*, "Parliament of Owls"; *Anomaly Literary Journal*, "Repurposing"; *SAND*, "Sognsvann"; *pif*, "Barn Sale"; *So It Goes*, "The New Canaan Village for Epileptics; *Juked*, "Masterpiece"; *Cold Mountain Review*, "The Shallow End; *Origins*, "Hiddenfolk"; *Hawai'i Pacific Review*, "Dick Fleming Is Lost."

NOTE FROM THE PUBLISHER

Thank you so much for purchasing *The Middle Ground* and supporting small press publishing and the arts. We truly appreciate it.

We hope you enjoyed reading *The Middle Ground*. We'd love to know how you found it. Please consider posting an honest review of the book on its Amazon and Goodreads pages, and/or anywhere else you wish. Aside from purchasing a book, reviews are the most effective way to support a writer. The quantity of reviews (positive or negative) of a book increases how many people discover that book, even if the reviews are just once sentence long.